M000202107

Naughty or Nice?

Also by Alison Tyler:

Best Bondage Erotica
Best Bondage Erotica 2
Exposed
The Happy Birthday Book of Erotica
Heat Wave: Sizzling Sex Stories
Luscious: Stories of Anal Eroticism
The Merry XXXmas Book of Erotica
Red Hot Erotica
Slave to Love
Three-Way
Caught Looking (with Rachel Kramer Bussel)
A Is for Amour
B Is for Bondage
C Is for Coeds
D Is for Dress-Up
E Is for Exotic
F Is for Fetish
G Is for Games
H Is for Hardcore
Got a Minute?
Love at First Sting
Hide and Seek (with Rachel Kramer Bussel)

Naughty or Nice?

Christmas Erotica

Edited by Alison Tyler

CLEIS
PRESS

Copyright © 2007 by Alison Tyler.

All rights reserved. Except for brief passages quoted in newspaper, magazine, radio, or television reviews, no part of this book may be reproduced in any form or by any means, electronic or mechanical, including photocopying or recording, or by information storage or retrieval system, without permission in writing from the publisher.

Published in the United States by Cleis Press Inc.,
P.O. Box 14697, San Francisco, California 94114.

Printed in the United States.
Cover design: Scott Idleman
Cover art: Getty
Text design: Frank Wiedemann
Cleis Press logo art: Juana Alicia
First Edition.
10 9 8 7 6 5 4 3 2 1

"Mulled Wine" by Dominic Santi was originally published in *Naughty Spanking Stories from A to Z, vol. 2,* edited by Rachel Kramer Bussel.

Acknowledgments

To those who make the naughty list every single year: Violet Blue, Kiki Bouche, Rachel Kramer Bussel, Eliza Castle, Kristina Lloyd, Mathilde Madden, Barbara Pizio, Thomas S. Roche, and to SAM, always.

"I used to be Snow White. But I drifted."
—Mae West

Contents

Introduction

I don't even have to ask, do I?

If you're reading this, if you're standing there with the book open in your hot little hands, then you have to admit to being among the naughty. But don't worry if your bright-red fishnet stockings are destined to be filled with coal each year, because naughty is the best way to be.

Why?

When you're naughty, you can leave a few extra buttons undone, revealing a glimpse of bare skin or a bit of racy lingerie. When you're naughty, you can hold a stranger's eye for an extra-long beat, imparting visions of twisted sex fantasies with your gaze alone. And when you're naughty, you can plunge yourself into the delicious confections created by the authors in this book—all of them just as naughty as you are! Or perhaps even naughtier still.

Check out Shanna Germain, for instance. Her character might pretend to be a good little girl. At least, at first. But when she goes before her lover who is dressed in drag as Santa, the truth comes out:

"I don't see you on my good list, though," Shannon pulled at her beard with one white-gloved hand. "Something tells me you were a bad girl this year."

"Oh, no, Santa, I was…" I didn't know what to say. Had I been good? And if so, was I going to get whatever I wanted? But if I was bad, then maybe I would have to be punished. I couldn't decide.

But it didn't matter, because Shannon was rubbing her gloved hands up my bare thighs. The fabric was soft and silky against my skin, and I imagined her pressing the tips to my clit, rubbing, soaking up my juices. She was whispering in my ear, her beard scratching against my skin, "I think you were a very bad girl, don't you?"

In "Carol's Christmas," Lisette Ashton retells the famed *A Christmas Carol* by Charles Dickens. Unfortunately, Carol doesn't learn from the lessons shown to her by the Ghost of Christmas Future. But that doesn't mean she won't get what she wants for Christmas:

She laughed giddily and allowed another rush of glorious satisfaction to quiver through her frame. She had been blessed with a glimpse of a bleak and agonizing future, and she couldn't wait to experience every one of the painful torments she had been shown.

Being naughty can add spice to any relationship, as deliciously displayed in Dominic Santi's humorously sexy "Mulled Wine":

"Why does your dick taste like mulled wine?"

If Glen and I were monogamous, that would be a problem. Fortunately, we're not. So I grinned when I looked down at him and said, "I stopped at Jake and Karl's Christmas party on the way home."

"Oh, indeed!" Glen leaned forward, once more sucking my dick into his mouth. His short blond curls bobbed against his Santa hat, and his blue eyes twinkled up at me. He sucked me long and slowly, like he was drawing the flavor off my skin to differentiate each of the specific tastes. "Cinnamon, clove," he laughed, pulling back for a moment. "Perhaps a hint of allspice…"

In my opinion, life doesn't get much naughtier than performing a taste test for exotic spices on your lover's cock. And as the Queen of Naughty, I should know.

So pour your own goblet of mulled wine, find a willing partner, and get ready to do a taste test of your own. Or at least find someone willing to listen to a few X-rated Xmas tales.

Wishing you a truly naughty holiday season,

Alison Tyler

The Queen of Christmas
Andrea Dale

They called me the Queen of Christmas. I was the Queen of Christmas.

I was the one who organized the carolers in full, proper Victorian clothing. I was the one who welcomed other caroling groups with wassail, candy canes, and stockings (lovingly hand-embroidered) stuffed with goodies. I was the one who liberated the Nativity scene that the city was retiring, so I was the one with life-size camels in my front yard. I was the one with the lighted, moving reindeer on the roof and the Santa who moved up and down the chimney.

People came from miles around to see what the Queen of Christmas had in store this year.

That is, until *he* moved across the street.

He went pretty elaborate for Halloween, and I thought, "Fine, that's your holiday." But then Christmas rolled around.

At first, his display seemed innocuous: Mostly lights. Lots of them but all white. He might illuminate the neighborhood like it was midday, but all the better to see my yard, you know?

Then one night I heard the music. He'd cleverly hidden some impressive speakers in the bushes, because I could hear the tunes with the window closed and the carols on my own stereo. So help me, my china rattled.

We've all seen the Trans-Siberian Orchestra house, right? He'd recreated the damn thing. Impressive, yes. But it was seriously detracting from my own decorations.

So I went over there and hammered on his front door, making his cranberry-and-ivy wreath bounce against the wood.

"Oh, hey, Shelly," he said.

Of course, he knew who I was. On December 1, I deliver plates of hand-decorated sugar cookies to everyone in the neighborhood and then, on the fifth, a schedule of all of the local schools' pageants and concerts, printed on fir-scented paper. On the fifteenth, gingerbread men and eggnog. On the twenty-first, solstice candles and, at the appropriate time, oil for Hanukkah. (Never let it be said I don't respect all of the winter holidays.)

See, now here's the other problem. I'd had my eye on Bradley St. Clair since the moment he moved into the neighborhood. He's one yummy-looking man, and he had my panties damp from the start. I'd done some flirting, but I was waiting to make my move until after Twelfth Night, when things calmed down again. That didn't mean I hadn't masturbated more than once thinking about him, and I'd even dusted off a pair of binoculars to find how much I could see across the street.

Sadly, his bedroom was at the back of the house, and I was not enough of a Peeping Tom to hide in his backyard bushes.

Right now, he had on a long-underwear top with a convenient tear highlighting his chest and faded jeans that molded to his muscular thighs. Casual but oh-so-sexy. He held a snifter of brandy in one hand, and his dark hair was rumpled.

For a long moment, I forgot why I'd stormed over there. I forgot that I'd stormed, even. I was too busy staring at him, my nipples at greater attention than the tin soldiers in "The Nutcracker." Salute me, baby.

Then I realized he was talking, and I couldn't hear him over that damnable music.

"Turn it down!" I shouted.

"What? Oh, right." He turned a knob just inside the front door, and the orchestra from hell retreated a few thousand decibels.

"C'mon in," he said. "Want some brandy?"

Well, damn, I wasn't about to turn that down.

"That's some display," I said as he poured my drink. I meant the lights and music, but the sight of his fine ass as he bent over to pick up the cap he'd dropped was something to behold.

"Thanks," he said. He handed me the drink and sat down next to me. He smelled kind of piney, kind of cinnamony. Like Christmas. I squirmed in my seat. It was hot in here, and not just from the fire crackling in the fireplace. "I've been working on the specs for a couple of years," he continued. "The electrical engineering degree finally came in handy for something interesting."

"It's really loud," I said, cursing myself for sounding like someone's mother at a rock concert.

"Yeah, sorry about that. I'm still smoothing out the details. I didn't realize how far the sound carried." He didn't look abashed or repentant, although I didn't doubt the sincerity of his apology. He was simply acknowledging his mistake, confident that he could fix the problem.

Maybe it was the brandy, or the heat off his tight bod, or the glint of a tiny gold hoop in his right ear. Whatever. I accepted his apology, and I don't remember much of the conversation after that. Something about our mutual love of the season. He liked my chimney-climbing Santa, was impressed by my mechanical ability. Cool. Go me. Do you mind if I lean in and just inhale you?

I caught myself before I did anything stupid. I had the holidays to get through before I could allow myself to move into full-on seduction mode. And besides, he was still pissing me off a little.

Best intentions and all that. I was standing in his foyer, pulling on my faux-fur-cuffed leather gloves for the chilly tromp across the street, when I clued in to his wolfish grin.

"What?"

He tilted his head up.

I followed his gaze, and saw the mistletoe dangling from the amber Arts-and-Crafts light fixture. Aw, hell.

He kissed with the same confidence he'd shown when talking about his engineering expertise. One hand loosely threaded through my hair, keeping me against him. His lips moved against mine, his teeth nipping my lower lip and then his tongue darting out to soothe.

I felt that kiss all the way down to my clit, and then some.

I was pretty much ready to hop up and wrap my legs around his waist in preparation for him carrying me off to some soft surface where he could ring my jingle bells, when he eased away.

"Happy holidays, Shelly," he said.

Oh, yeah, I was sure they'd be happy, all right. And once they were over…

Once they were over, I was simply going to have to kill him. Call it the candy-cane defense.

True to his word, Bradley kept the music to a reasonable level. His impressive decorations had something to do with the increase in the number of people visiting our street, and it irked the hell out of me to stand on my front porch in a holly-patterned apron with a tray of green-and-red sparkled cupcakes and face everyone's backs.

And then there was the line to get into his backyard. What in Jesus' birthday was that all about?

I'll tell you. I went over and found out he'd set up a whole Santa's Grotto, and dressed himself as Santa. He had a huge bag of gifts, and he didn't discriminate about who got them.

That wasn't all. He had a slide—a slide—for kids to skim down to land right next to ol' Santa.

He had completely, utterly, totally gazumped everything I'd ever done.

And he was going to pay.

In my defense, he started it. It was his mistletoe, and he kissed me.

That's what gave me the idea. I had to find a way through his defenses; I had to hit him where it hurt. Which, I realized, was below the belt.

Santa could not work effectively with a boner is what I'm saying.

I went for less of a Mrs. Claus look and more of a Santa's helper theme. Skimpy white-fur-trimmed, red stretch-velvet top and flippy, short velvet skirt. Wide black belt cinching my waist in an attractive fashion. Black fishnet thigh-highs and short black boots with a sassy heel.

To top it all off, a perky Santa hat with a pin that said, MISTLETOE: KISS BELOW.

The plan was simple: Distract him, and then offer him the goods only if he backed down from the contest. Hopefully, it wouldn't take too long because in this outfit, I was going to freeze my cute buns off very quickly.

I loaded up a basket of cookies and made my way across the street, my boots crunching in the snow at the curb. There was a line of people all down the sidewalk, waiting to get back there. I smiled at them, and they parted to let me through, assuming I was part of the show.

I waited until a kid came out of the grotto, and popped inside before Brad could call for the next one to come down the slide.

"Shelly!" He stood when he saw me. "I'd say 'ho-ho-ho,' but I wouldn't want you to take it the wrong way."

"You like?" I asked, pirouetting to give him a full view.

"I do, indeed," he said. "But why are you here?"

"What do you mean?"

"It's obvious that you can't stand the competition—that you hate anyone having what might be construed as a better holiday display."

I'd always thought jaw-dropping was a cliché, but mine did. I'd had no freaking clue he knew how I felt.

"I've always had the house everyone talks about," I said. "It's my thing."

He shook his head. Even with the padded suit and the wig and the poufy white eyebrows, he was still majorly hot, and that tingle I was feeling wasn't from the cold. "Christmas is about sharing, about giving."

"So back off."

"Can't we both have great displays?"

I didn't want him to be reasonable. It made me feel unreasonable. And unseasonable. "No," I said stubbornly.

I knew I was being pouty. I knew I deserved coal in my stocking. But I was still surprised when Brad snatched me up and sat down on his throne with me head down and ass up.

I started to say something about this not being the appropriate way to sit on Santa's lap when his hand connected with my now-very-vulnerable ass. I squealed as the pain and heat seared through me, knowing it was worse because my flesh was cold.

"Careful," Bradley said, his voice low and dark and dangerous. "You don't want the kiddies outside to hear."

As stubborn as I am, it's still about Christmas, and there was no way I'd risk spoiling Christmas for children. I squirmed, but I couldn't get any purchase, and Bradley's other hand was firmly in the small of my back. Another sharp smack, and I wondered whether that was audible over the cheerful holiday music. I assumed not, or he would've stopped. Somehow, I trusted that.

His hand came down on my ass again. I'd received play-spankings from partners in the past, but they'd never been my be-all, end-all.

This was entirely different.

Maybe it was the music, or the smell of spiced eggnog, or the crisp winter air. Probably all those things. It was definitely the fact that it was Santa's lap on which I was being thoroughly put in my place.

Three spanks in and I was completely, irretrievably aroused. Nipples hard like last year's fruitcake, my red stretch-lace panties drenched and my clit buzzing.

"Twelve," I dimly heard Brad say. "One for each day of Christmas."

Slap, slap, slap, and I was sure my ass was as red as the panties that covered it. I wanted him to pull them down; I wanted him to smell my arousal. I wanted him to search out my clit with his fingers and bring me over the edge, which I was sure would take only a stroke or two.

In the final flurry of smacks, I thought I might even come without the benefit of that. So close...

He stopped. Damn it. I could feel his erection pressing against my belly.

"Bradley..."

"The kids are waiting, Shell." He helped me to my feet, even though the last thing I wanted to do was stand up, and pointed to the basket of cookies I'd brought. "You can hand those out once they tell me what they want."

My cheeks flamed as red as my ass. He expected me to stand here, desperate for release, and make nice to the children as if nothing was going on?

Apparently so. Because he grinned that wolfish grin and added, "Then I'll give you what you really want."

He grabbed the pillow he'd used to cushion the wooden throne's seat and plopped it on his lap. Smart guy. Resourceful. Damn him.

No matter how much I resented him right now, I wanted my gift from Santa in the worst way. So I smiled and handed out cookies, constantly, achingly aware of the slickness between my thighs with every movement I made.

The kids were thrilled. Cranky as I was, I could see that. And a kid thrilled from meeting Santa went a long way to warm the cockles of the Queen of Christmas's heart. What could I do but succumb, even if I had to clutch the basket against my chest so they couldn't see my protruding nubs, even as I prayed the scent of gingerbread masked the scent of my own arousal.

By the time the last child toddled out of the grotto, I was light-headed from Christmas joy and joyous, desperate arousal.

"Wait here," Brad said. "I'll be right back."

Wait longer? I almost fainted from the thought. But I realized he was turning off the lights, making it clear that Santa's Grotto wasn't taking any new requests.

He reached for me, but I had other plans. Even as he kissed me hard enough to make my head spin, I nudged him backward until he was sitting on the throne again.

"You said Christmas was about giving, right?" I said, burrowing through the layers of padding and finally, blissfully, drawing out his cock. I sucked it like it was a candy cane and I was the starving Little Match Girl. I could've sworn he tasted like peppermint. I know he felt really good in my mouth, hard and sweet, and that his moans wove through and counterpointed the carols over the sound system like the tenor solo at church.

How could I never have come up with this kink before? Blowing Santa was bringing me closer to climax than being spanked by him.

We were both on the verge when, somehow, he found the strength to ease me off his cock. I whimpered with displeasure, but when he arranged me on my knees on the throne, my hands gripping the arm rests, I stopped complaining. I wiggled my ass invitingly, gazing over my shoulder at him.

He didn't need further invitation.

He sank into me, and when the crisp rough curls of his hair scraped against my sore, spanked ass, a shudder convulsed me.

Call it the Spirit of Christmas. All I know is that when Bradley started thrusting, the Queen of Christmas had met her match.

Fezziwig's Balls
Donna George Storey

It was becoming a tradition. Claire bought the tickets as soon as they went on sale in September. Robert booked the tower suite at the fancy bed-and-breakfast near the ballroom. In November, they splurged on private lessons to brush up on the schottische, mazurka, and, of course, the waltz. By the third year, they were even renting Victorian costumes for the occasion.

Claire didn't think of herself as the historical reenactor type, but the annual Fezziwig Ball brought out yearnings she didn't usually indulge at other seasons. The evening offered plenty to delight the senses: magnificent chandeliers twinkling like stars above the ballroom floor, a supper buffet laden with Christmas puddings and mince pies, the mellow pleasure of chatting and dancing with old friends at year's end. And, of course, the fact that afterward she and Robert went back to the inn and fucked themselves silly until dawn.

The first year, Robert came up behind her as she was gazing out the window at the city lights spread out below them. "Don't move. Don't say a word," he whispered and proceeded to lift her skirt and make love to her right there for any midnight passerby to see. The next year, Claire got the idea to play the virgin bride with Robert as her libertine husband intent on awakening her to every decadent pleasure the flesh could offer. The time after that, she cast him as the inattentive footman whose punishment was to crawl under Claire's hoopskirt and feast on his mistress's "quim" until she "spent"—not once but twice. Each year they pushed the boundaries just a bit further than the last. That was a tradition, too.

This October, when the leaves were just turning, Robert asked Claire to meet him after work at a certain address not far from the inn where they stayed the night of the ball. The sign above the old-fashioned doorbell was discreet: MADAME DOMINIQUE, CORSETIERE. However, the salon upstairs—where Robert sat waiting for her in a wingback chair, a glass of sherry in his hand—was a study in over-the-top bordello chic. The windows were hung with velvet draperies. The furnishings were rich mahogany, upholstered in baby-blue satin. A freestanding oval mirror occupied the center of the room, flanked by two headless mannequins. The one on the right wore a modest, cream-colored corset, the kind you see in BBC adaptations of Jane Austen novels. The other was the bad girl's choice: black leather bristling with metal studs, the front deeply scalloped to expose the breasts. Claire had never seen a mannequin with nipples like that—deep pink, eternally erect, and shimmering faintly as if they'd just been licked.

A small, blond woman of "a certain age" stepped out from the counter to greet her. Behind the cordial smile, Claire sensed calculation, as if Madame Dominique had already judged her waist size, how much she would spend, and exactly what kind of kinky scenes she would act out later with her husband while wearing her new purchase.

"May I offer you a glass of sherry before we begin the fitting?" Madame asked.

Claire glanced at Robert, who gave a curt nod.

"Yes, thank you," she murmured. She might not be as quick at reading people as Madame, but she knew her husband. He'd obviously promoted himself from last year's stint as her footman to imperious lord and master.

No doubt he meant for her to be tipsy when she slipped behind the Chinese screen to change into the undergarments Madame provided. The pantalets were comfortable enough. The chemise, however, was stiff with starch, and it chafed Claire's sensitive nipples. To her embarrassment, they poked up provocatively through the thin cloth, rather like the whorish mannequin's. Instinctively, she crossed her arms over her chest as she stepped back out into the room.

Both heads turned toward her. Robert's eyes glided down her body and then up again. Madame smiled and guided her over to the mirror, her hand warm against Claire's back.

"We'll begin the fitting now, so I must ask you to lower your arms, please, Mrs. Ryan. There's no need to be shy," she said in a soothing voice. "Mr. Ryan informed me you'll be wearing this as the foundation for a ball gown from the mid-Victorian period, so, of course, I've selected the historically appropriate style."

Claire glanced at the corset in Madame's hands, a pale pink version of the one the "nice girl" mannequin was wearing. She felt a pang of disappointment. Part of her wanted to be the whore, wrapped tight in slick leather, tits exposed. On the other hand, the virgin-on-her-wedding-night scene proved well enough that playing the submissive wife brought its own satisfactions.

With a nervous smile, she lowered her arms. Madame wrapped the corset around Claire's torso and quickly fastened the clasps in front. Then she circled behind to tighten the laces. With each tug, Claire felt her chest move forward and up in response. The corset seemed to embrace her, meld itself to her skin, squeezing her breath and her flesh vertically so that she felt inches taller.

She also felt an undeniable twinge of pleasure between her legs.

"It's not too tight, is it?" Madame asked, her voice almost a whisper.

"No, it's fine," Claire responded, her own voice faint and breathless. For the first time she allowed herself to take in her full image in the mirror: the flushed cheeks, the pinched waist and voluptuous flaring of her hips, the shadow of dark hair between her legs through almost-translucent pantalets. Beside her in the mirror floated Robert's face, his eyes glued to her perfect hourglass form.

"Lovely," Madame breathed, resting her hands on Claire's hips. "This suits you very well. Your figure is just full enough for a charming décolletage."

As she spoke, Madame's fingers glided upward over the boning of the corset. Claire held her breath. Surely the woman would not be so bold as to touch a customer's breasts, if only to emphasize a compliment?

She had underestimated the corsetiere. For just an instant her fingers grazed Claire's nipples, lightly, discreetly, before they pulled away.

Claire stiffened. She would have guessed the corset would provide a barrier to a stolen caress, but the satin—and the tightness—seemed to amplify the sensation. She glanced up and caught Madame's gaze in the mirror. The woman had the brazenness to smile.

"This is just the thing for Fezziwig's Ball, don't you think?" Robert's voice was husky. He cleared his throat. "Can you have the order ready by the middle of December?"

"Is this a Christmas present for your wife, then? How charming," Madame cooed.

Claire watched the Robert in the mirror incline his head stiffly. He was playing his part well—the tight-buttoned Victorian gentleman, giving nothing away—although all three of them knew that certain gifts can bring equal pleasure to the giver as well.

A four-hundred-dollar corset was only the beginning of Robert's Yuletide bounty. At his request, Madame introduced them to a seamstress who specialized in historical costumes. After much discussion, Claire settled on a lavish ball gown of cornflower blue. As she stood through the endless fittings, she did wonder now and then if historical accuracy was worth all the trouble and expense.

Until the night of Fezziwig's Ball.

Like most reasonably attractive women, Claire had experienced her share of lustful glances, but never had she felt so admired, so seen. No man, whether friend or stranger, could keep his eyes from devouring her shapely bosom, her tiny waist. The women's gazes were even hungrier. They drank in the yards of shimmering silk and the nosegay of fresh flowers tucked in her sash as they might drool over a cup of frothy hot chocolate from a Viennese konditorei. Claire's dance card filled quickly. She even yielded a few to strangers who asked for the favor of her company. She could hardly turn down the president of the Dickens Society himself, and a very young man who'd dressed up as a Union general asked so gallantly, she couldn't refuse.

The first dance, of course, was with her husband.

"How are you feeling in that corset?" he asked as they took their first turn past the orchestra.

"A little dizzy, even though I haven't had any Christmas punch. I'm sure I'll be more than ready to take it off once we get out of here."

"That can be arranged." Robert pulled her closer.

"How does it feel to you?"

"Interesting. It's you but it's not. It's like touching a doll, something man-made. To tell the truth, I miss the sensation of flesh."

"Don't worry, I'm still alive in here." Claire was about to confess that his touch through the corset was oddly arousing, as if he were stroking her skin with satin gloves. But, she decided, there would be plenty of time for truth later, when the corset came off.

"You look ravishing, Claire," their friend Paul said, bending over her gloved hand with a courtly flourish. "How did you manage to talk that skinflint husband of yours into springing for this get-up?"

"Actually, it was Robert's idea."

"Really? I didn't think he had it in him."

But when Paul took her in his arms for the dance, his smirk turned quickly to a look of surprise.

"Yes, I'm wearing a real corset. I'm historically accurate down to the lacy drawers with the split crotch."

"What's next, then? Reenacting Civil War battles every weekend?"

"You laugh, but you might be interested to know that historical reenactors are notorious spouse swappers. It makes sense. They are experts at bringing fantasies to life."

"Then please let me do what I can to encourage your new hobby," he replied with a twinkle in his eye. "I think I understand your husband's motives better now. But still, the outfit must have cost him a fortune."

"Don't you think I'm worth it?"

"I have no doubt you command the highest price."

They'd always flirted shamelessly, and it seemed innocent enough to Claire—that is, until tonight. It wasn't just that Paul kept staring at her cleavage, or even that he couldn't stop moving his hand over her bodice, fingering the boning and laces with obvious excitement. It was her own reaction that troubled her. She always found dancing with another man strangely intimate. If only for a few moments, she was captive to his rhythm, the heat or coolness of his hands, the smell of him—aftershave, sweat, or breath mints, if he was really insecure. But this time it was more, as if Paul were flashing images through his hands, through the corset, the obscene vision of her own body laid out on a bed in her corset and bloomers. Paul was there, too, bending over to kiss her breasts, his hand snaking through the gap in the crotch of the pantalets to strum her clit and coax out the sweet music of her moans.

Fortunately, the next dance was Robert's, and in truth, she looked forward to his sober, conjugal company to save her from herself.

Five minutes later, her husband was still nowhere to be seen. Not that she minded. The dance with Paul left her winded, her bosom heaving like a heroine's in a romance novel. When Robert did show up, she planned on begging him to let her sit this one out.

"If you'll forgive the intrusion, madam." A deep voice, faintly accented, slipped into her ear like warm syrup. Claire turned. A gray-haired man in white tie and tails stood beside her. He was not much taller than she and elegantly slim. With another quick glance she took in his white gloves, the blue blood's aquiline nose.

"If I didn't know better, I'd swear you stepped straight out of Dickens."

The man's accent was too perfect for a nineteenth-century ball. She guessed Central Europe—Vienna or Budapest, perhaps. Was it real? Did it matter? She nodded graciously to accept the compliment.

He bowed in return. "May I inquire if you are free for the next dance?"

Claire was about to make her excuses, but at that moment the orchestra struck up the opening notes of "The Blue Danube," and there was still no sign of Robert. He could hardly hold it against her if she chose a dance over the dreaded fate of wallflower.

Offering his arm, the man led her straight to the center of the floor. Bowing once more, he took her up in his arms. "Up" was exactly the word, for suddenly Claire was floating, her body turning and gliding at the faintest pressure of his hand. She had never danced with a partner who so clearly knew what he was doing, who could transport her to a place where she was no longer beholden to gravity, only to his whim. Was it his whim, then, that her nipples were throbbing under their satin casing and the secret place between her legs was tingling and distressingly wet? She didn't even need to imagine his spit-moistened palms making slow circles over her breasts, or the way he'd gallantly slip a pillow under her ass before he fucked her, or any of the other time-honored tricks the rakes of the Old World used to seduce married ladies from the path of virtue. The intoxicating whirl of the dance was enough.

Afterward, she had to lean against him for a moment to get her bearings. Knees wobbling, her face hot and flushed, if she hadn't had an actual orgasm, she probably looked as if she had. It was then she saw Robert, watching, eyes narrowed, a cool smile of triumph playing over his lips.

"Admit it, Claire, you enjoyed it. Far too much for a proper wife." Robert's voice was stern as he stood over her in the darkness of their room.

At first she tried to be modern and lighthearted. "Oh, come on. The guy must have been thirty years older than me. And he talked funny, too."

"Don't bore me with excuses. Did you like dancing with him?"

Claire lowered her gaze. It was strange how the pose alone made her feel guilty, contrite. Her pussy muscles clenched, arousal mixed with fear. Even if Robert hadn't planned this from the start, he was taking full advantage of an incriminating circumstance.

What could a lady do, but follow her husband's lead?

"Yes, I did like it," she said softly.

"Just as I suspected. Now, I want you to lie back on the bed and lift your skirt like the whore you are."

She flinched at the word, although in her twenty-first-century life, she had a feminist's respect for any woman's free choice to engage in sex work. But tonight her hands shook with Victorian shame as she gathered the skirt and petticoat in her hands and lay back on the soft mattress.

"Spread your legs and show me your twat through that very convenient slit in your drawers. No need to feign modesty. You were willing enough to show off the goods for those men tonight. I'm sure it gave you quite a 'stirring in your loins.'"

She tried to protest, but all that came out was a whimper.

Robert probed her pussy lips, none too gently. "Ah, yes, the body never lies. You're all slick and ready for a big, hard cock. Will mine do, or shall I call in your European lover to do the honors?"

"I want you to make love to me, Robert. Please," she managed to bleat out.

"Spoken like the slut you are. No lady wants it so bad she begs for it. Look at you, you're even panting."

"It's the corset. It's hard to breathe. Can you help me take it off?"

"In good time, my dear. First, I want to watch you come while you're wearing it."

She gulped. "I might faint."

"That's exactly what I had in mind, my little whore. I want to make you come so hard you'll black out all the other men who had you tonight."

Claire heard the rustle of cloth as he struggled out of his trousers. With no further preliminaries, he guided the head of his cock to her swollen cunt lips and pushed inside. Through her daze, Claire marveled at the perfection of the setting. The four-poster bed was just the right height for a stand-up fuck, and her position—thighs spread wide across the mattress—gave him easy access to her clit, a situation Robert immediately exploited.

Claire moaned and crossed her ankles behind his waist. It was true. She had enjoyed the glittering stares, the excitement pulsing through her partners' hands, and most of all the consummate skill of that mysterious stranger who made her fly through the air. Maybe she was a trollop, willing to be handled and defiled by any man who gave her the time of day. But what about Robert? He might be proper and priggish from the waist up, but down below he was nothing more than a rutting beast, ramming his dick inside her all the way up to his family jewels.

Not that she minded that, either, because with each thrust his balls were rubbing up against her nether parts in the most stimulating way. She wriggled her ass to open herself wider, as if she were doing a little jig on the mattress. Suddenly the strangest vision danced before her eyes: round Mr. Fezziwig, capering across the warehouse floor with his wife, bringing cheer to kith and kin each year with his merry Yuletide balls.

She would have laughed if she hadn't been so turned on. Robert was acquitting himself most worthily in his marital duty, fingering her clit, filling her cunt with his manhood, tickling her asshole with his own jolly, bouncing balls. And now he had one more surprise. His hand traveled to her bosom, seeking her nipple through the layers of ball gown and corset.

She gasped and arched off the bed. She could feel her nipples stiffen, but the pressure of the corset forced the sensation inward, electric jolts of pleasure that radiated through the satin. Her whole torso was burning, melting. She thrashed and twisted, but Robert stayed with her, his balls lodged in her ass crack, his finger flicking her clit in quick time.

"Fuck me, oh, yes," she babbled, grinding herself against him in the most wanton manner.

"Then show me how much you love it. Come on my cock right now," Robert growled.

Of course, a lady had no choice but to obey her husband.

Except no one could call her a lady now. She was a fallen woman, tumbling through space, her orgasm shooting from deep inside her belly and up through the corset to burst from her throat in a scream of release.

Robert emptied himself into her with a bestial cry of his own.

"How was that for a last dance of the Dickens Ball?" His voice was his own, soft and sated.

"It was the climax of the evening," she said with a smile. And yes, it would be a tough act to follow, but she already had a few plans for next year. She'd buy him the most elegant and authentic costume, down to the sock garters and a dashing white chemise, then bring him to his knees. She wasn't quite sure how, but she knew it would work out fine if she just put her faith in the Ghost of Christmas Yet To Come.

It was becoming a tradition.

A Good Little Girl
Shanna Germain

"Daria's Delights. This is Kay—how may I help you?"

"I got a job," Shannon's voice on the phone was a pleasant relief from a crazy morning of pre-Christmas underwear sales.

"Holy shit!" I said. The man standing at the counter looked up from the string-of-pearl thong he was holding. "Sorry," I said to him. He nodded and went back to trying to decide between pearl and chain.

Into the phone, a little softer, I said, "Shan, that's awesome. I'm so proud of you."

She laughed. Shannon's got a big, boisterous laugh that I love. "It's just a seasonal gig."

"Who cares," I said. "Tell me all about it."

"Can't. It's a surprise." Shannon sounded more like her old self than she had since she'd been laid off from work a few months ago. Since then, she'd tried to find temporary holiday work but had mainly been sulking around the house and scrubbing things out of guilt for not bringing in any money.

"Meet me tonight and I'll show you," she said. "I'll leave directions on the bed."

After I hung up the phone, I couldn't stop smiling, even though the man didn't buy anything. Directions on the bed? That was our longtime term for an evening of fun, but we hadn't had the money—or the desire—to do anything in a while.

All day long, as I wrapped lacy thongs destined for Christmas gifts, I tried to figure out what kind of job she'd gotten that would entail directions on the bed. I couldn't imagine her bartending. She was too honest to kiss the asses of drunken business men. And I doubted she'd be dancing topless— Shannon's built more like a barrel than a Barbie. I personally love her thick thighs and round belly, but I doubted that was the look most dollar-stuffers were going for.

As soon as my shift was over, I ran home to see what she'd left me. Spread out on the bed was a girly miniskirt with a white baby-doll T. "Pigtails are good. Clean-shaven is also good," she'd written on the sticky note on top of my tennis shoes. "See you soon."

I hopped in the shower for a quick rinse and shave. Clean-shaven meant I'd most likely be getting at least semi-naked in front of others soon. Shannon knew there were few things I loved more than fucking her in public. I didn't know how that worked into her new job. Maybe it didn't. Maybe I was just going to pick her up and we'd go somewhere after.

In the bedroom, I pulled everything on, including a pair of boy-cut panties, then took a look in the mirror. The short blue skirt showed my long legs nearly to the bottom of my ass, and the T-shirt Shannon had picked out was so tight it highlighted my small boobs. Jesus, I looked about sixteen. I completed the look with a smear of shiny lip gloss.

The bad news was that my legs were bare. Shit, I was going to be freezing my ass off. Didn't she realize it was the middle of December?

I pulled my down coat out of the closet—I looked like a lollipop wrapped in a marshmallow, but at least I'd be warm in the car. I'd take it off when I got there. Maybe. I still wasn't sure where there was, although Shannon had printed out a Yahoo map for me.

The drive wasn't far—it only took me about twenty minutes. But I was pretty sure I'd taken a wrong turn. Up and down the street, only big, quiet old houses. What was the deal? Was Shannon house-sitting somewhere? Hopefully, she wasn't babysitting—she loved kids, but, man, after an hour with her nieces and nephews, she had them all on sugar highs and jumping off the furniture.

I parked the car at the end of the block and threw my coat into the backseat. Shivering, I counted house numbers. I didn't need to: even before I got to the address, I could see the party lights and hear the tinny sound of holiday music.

Great, I thought, she's serving cocktails for some haughty old folks, and I'm supposed to show up looking like Gidget's baby sister. How does she get me into these things?

But it was way too cold to be standing in the driveway worrying, so I ran up to the front door and rang the bell. An elf—about my height and with the most gorgeous green eyes I'd ever seen—opened the door.

"Welcome to the Jingle No-Ball!" she said, sweeping her bell-clad arm around the room.

"Th-thanks," I shivered. The whole place looked like

something out of the North Pole—there was fake snow everywhere, cotton running in drifts along the floor, and elves rushing around carrying plates of cookies.

"Make yourself at home," the elf said with a wink, as she closed the door behind me.

The other guests were in the living room, milling around with food and drinks. To my relief, I saw that I wasn't the only one dressed up. There were lots and lots of grown-ups in little-girl outfits—a few even wore footed pajamas and carried teddy bears. I looked at my bare legs and cursed Shannon for not thinking of that, instead. Others wore antlers and red noses, or gift wrapping. I didn't see any real boys, although there were at least a few girls who were packing, dressed in sailor suits or as boy elves.

I took a quick look around for Shannon but didn't see her. At least, I knew from everyone else's costumes that I was at the right house. I didn't see her in the dining room, either, which was filled with all kinds of finger foods and steaming bowls of cider and eggnog. I poured myself a cup of eggnog—it was brandy-warm and delicious.

Through the kitchen was another room, a sort of second living room with a huge fireplace and sparkling tree loaded with presents. Girls and reindeer sat on couches and chairs, while elves ran to and fro with a seemingly endless supply of food.

And, there, in the middle of it all, in a huge royal chair, was Santa. I took a couple of steps closer and realized it wasn't Santa, it was Shannon.

She wore typical garb: red suit, a white wig that covered her blond stubble, and a white beard. Her big belly pressed against the front of her suit, filled it in a way that made it obvious that she hadn't had to stuff it—it was all her. She was the most beautiful Santa I'd ever seen. I was getting wet, just watching her sit there in her fluffy red suit. I'd never wanted to sit on Santa's lap so badly in my life.

There was already someone on her lap, though—and a whole line of girls waiting for her. I could tell just by looking that they weren't all good girls, either. I wanted to give them a shove out of the way and join the bad-girl list myself. But instead, I got in line behind a pig-tailed redhead in pink pj's. She was sucking on a candy cane, and it was turning her lips as red as Rudolph's nose.

I couldn't remember the last time I'd had a candy cane. Working in retail during the holidays for so many years—listening to "Jingle Bells" thirty times a day and putting out decorations in October—had quenched a lot of the joy I'd once had about Christmas.

I gave the girl a smile, and she smiled back around the candy cane, showing teeth that were a Christmas-y shade of pink.

"Hey, where did you get that?" I don't know why I whispered. It just felt right.

She ducked her head toward me. "My mommy put it in my stocking," she said. Then she pulled another one out of her pajama pants pocket and held it out to me. "Mommy says I should share."

"Wow, thanks," I said. "I like these."

"Me, too," she said.

We stood, sucking on our candy canes, waiting for the line to move. It wasn't going very fast, though; everyone seemed to be having a great time on Shannon's lap. And she was the perfect Santa; I could hear her ho-ho-ho's from where I stood in line, and saw her give more than a few girls a swat on the behind as they climbed off her lap.

I tried not to get antsy, but watching Shannon, waiting for

her, made my insides all wiggly. I sucked harder on my candy cane, trying to let the mint take over my mouth and distract me from what I really wanted.

Finally, it was the redheaded girl's turn, which meant I was next. I tried not to look as the girl plopped herself down on Shannon's lap. I couldn't hear what they were saying, but I did hear Shannon tell her she could have whatever she wanted and then give that big belly laugh.

I was already wet under my skirt and wishing I hadn't worn panties. Would Shannon be able to get her hands up there? I didn't know, but that was all I cared about.

After a few minutes, the redhead jumped off Shannon's lap and gave her a kiss on the cheek. "Thank you, Santa," she said. Then she flashed me another pink-toothed grin and stood at the side of the chair.

It was my turn, and I suddenly got shy. I sidled up to her, my head down. "Hi, Santa," I whispered.

Shannon opened her arms wide and said "ho-ho-ho!" in a way that made it sound less like she was laughing and more like she knew exactly what was on my mind.

I jumped into her lap, and she wrapped those big arms around me and pulled me to her. Her belly was so soft, wrapped in the velvety costume. The beard and hair hid her face really well—the only way I could tell it was Shannon's face was by her big brown eyes looking at me.

As I settled in her lap, I realized she was packing—something long and large from the feel of it. The pressure of it against me was incredible—it was all I could do to keep myself from wiggling around like jelly.

"And what would you like from Santa, little girl?" Shannon asked with a mischievous twinkle in her eyes as she jiggled her hips beneath me.

"I, uh, would, uh…" The unexpected pleasure of the dildo wiggling beneath me made it hard to concentrate. I could feel it rubbing against the thin fabric of my skirt, like it wanted to work its way inside.

"I don't see you on my good list, though," Shannon pulled at her beard with one white-gloved hand. "Something tells me you were a bad girl this year."

"Oh, no, Santa, I was…" I didn't know what to say. Had I been good? And if so, was I going to get whatever I wanted? But if I was bad, then maybe I would have to be punished. I couldn't decide.

But it didn't matter, because Shannon was rubbing her gloved hands up my bare thighs. The fabric was soft and silky against my skin, and I imagined her touching my clit, rubbing, soaking up my juices. She whispered in my ear, her beard scratching against my skin. "I think you were a very bad girl, don't you?"

I nodded. I didn't trust myself to speak. And I didn't want to open my eyes—I knew there were other little girls and elves who wanted Santa's attention, but I didn't want to share. I guess that made me a bad girl after all.

Shannon's hands were pulling the skirt up, seeking out my center, and I inched toward the edge of her lap, feeling the dildo slide along my crack. I wanted her to slide her hands under my panties and touch me with those perfect white gloves—I could just imagine them, starting with slow circles, then growing more insistent.

Shannon gave the inside of my thigh a slap. "Bad girls don't get what they ask for, you know that, right?"

"But…" I said.

"The only butt in this story is yours," she said. "Now, hop off Santa's lap."

"I don't want to," I said. I put my lips out in a big, candy-cane–coated pout.

"Well, then you'd better get on Santa's good list, don't you think?" She stood, tumbling me off her lap. Then she un-buckled her big square black belt. I went down on my knees in front of her and opened my mouth, begging for her to stuff my throat. I wanted to suck her so badly, I could already taste the rubber. Out of the corner of my eye, I could see the redhead sucking on her candy cane hard, one hand down the front of her pink pj's.

In front of me, Shannon opened the crotch of the Santa pants and brought out the dildo. She must have picked it up earlier, or else it came as part of the job. It was bright green and ridged like a long, thin Christmas tree.

She offered it up to me, and I sucked it the way I'd sucked the candy cane. I loved the feel of the rubber against my teeth, the thrust of her hips, the way she grabbed the back of my head like she'd never let go. I moaned against the rubber as her thrusts increased and she forced herself farther back in my throat.

She pulled away from me before I was ready, leaving me with my mouth empty and my clit beating jingle bells against the stupid panties I'd worn.

I stood. My panties were soaked, my mouth tasted like rubber and mint, and I could feel the line of girls behind me waiting their turn.

Shannon sat back down in the Santa throne and steadied the dildo with her hand. "Now, you can come sit on Santa's lap," she said.

I climbed back on her, catching a glimpse of the redhead next to us, who had gotten rid of her candy cane and had both hands down her pajama bottoms.

Shannon put her hands on my hips. "Turn around," Shannon said. I turned and looked out into the living room. Everywhere, there were girl couples, sharing couches and floor space. A few girls sat in the corners watching, their hands busy across their bodies. In the Santa line, girls watched us, touching themselves inside skirts and pajamas. One of the girls whose outfit—the zip-up pj's with feet—I'd coveted earlier was struggling with her zipper. I'd never been so glad to be in a miniskirt.

Shannon bent me over a bit and pushed the crotch of my underwear to one side, exposing my shaven pussy to the air. Then she positioned me over the dildo, teasing the tip in and out of my lips.

"Please…" I couldn't help whispering—I wanted her inside me.

"Please what?" She pulled the back of my panties down as she spoke.

"Please, Santa," I said. She slid the dildo in just a little, and I gasped. "Please, please, I'll be good, I'll be a good girl," I said.

When I said "girl," Shannon pressed me down on the dildo all the way. I was so wet, it slid up inside me without stopping, and then Shannon had both hands on my bare ass and was forcing me up and down. The slippery rubber inside me, combined with the soft fur of her suit, was driving me over the edge. The chair was so high up it was like I was looking down on all those people fucking around us. And with Shannon driving the dildo in and out of me, all I could think was "This must be what it's like for those angels on top of the tree. Heaven."

Without stopping, Shannon said, "Okay, little girl. Let's make your wish come true."

At first, I thought she was talking to me. "But you don't know what—"

But she was talking to the redhead, who had pulled her hands out of her jammies and was stepping up in front of the chair. "Really?" the girl asked. She had her hands behind her back, and her head down, just like when she'd given me the candy cane.

"Ho-ho-ho, baby," Shannon said. "Really."

The redhead reached out and lifted my baby-doll T. Then she leaned over and put her warm, wet, sticky mouth on my nipple. A spark popped somewhere between my nipple and my clit. Or maybe it was in my head. All I could do was moan and keep riding Santa's big green dildo.

Then, with the other hand, the redhead gently touched my exposed clit.

"Jesus," I breathed. My vision was blurred, but all around me I could see girls with their hands on each other, moving in the same rhythm as I.

As we moved together, the three of us, the redhead got bolder with her fingers, stroking my clit harder and harder. She tugged at my nipple with her teeth, and I gulped air, trying to hold on, but I knew I was getting too close to back down and wait. The room was spinning. From the sounds Shannon was making behind me, I knew she was feeling the same way. She bucked beneath me, sending her dick into me again and again.

Pleasure took over, a three-pronged star of nipple, clit, and insides. For a few seconds, I was lost in a whiteout, feeling only my own body as I came.

A few minutes later, I was dripping wet, covered in sweat and my own juices, feeling Shannon sigh against my neck. The redhead in front of me gave me one last smile and hopped away into the crowd of girls. A few of the girls in line yelled, "We want to see Santa, too!"

But before she let me up, Shannon whispered in my ear, "Did you get your wish, little girl?"

"No." I pouted my big lip again. "I want Santa to come every day."

"He can," she said. "I get to keep the suit."

Carol's Christmas
Lisette Ashton

> *"Ghost of the Future!" he exclaimed, "I fear you more than any spectre I have seen. But as I know your purpose is to do me good, and as I hope to live to be another man from what I was, I am prepared to bear you company, and do it with a thankful heart. Will you not speak to me?"*
> —A *Christmas Carol,* Charles Dickens (1843)

It had been a strange night. Perhaps the strangest of her life—although she conceded that was a pretty tight judgment call. No one dabbles with BDSM, humiliation, and bondage without garnering a few piquant memories. But with a succession of ghosts, visitations, and warnings to mend her errant ways, Carol had to admit this ranked high on the list of her remarkable nights. It was certainly the most surreal way she had ever spent a Christmas Eve. She pulled at the cuffs holding her wrists and ankles to the corners of the bedposts.

They remained tight.

Secure.

Inescapable.

Her naked body glistened with an unseasonable sheen of perspiration. In the moonlight that filtered through the bedroom window she could see her flesh sparkled like the glossiest of glossy Christmas wrapping paper. It was a monochrome scene: beautifully lit but bereft of color. Her bare breasts were tipped by rigid nipples. Hard. Fat. Sensitive. Her shaved pussy was a softly pouting mouth. Her chest pounded with the familiar sensations of adrenaline, excitement, and a heartfelt fear of the unknown.

"I am in the presence of the Ghost of Christmas Yet To Come?"

The spirit said nothing.

"Shit!" she thought. "The strong-and-silent-type." They were the men who always inspired her most depraved appetites. Her breathing deepened. The knowledge she was bound, naked, and helpless beneath the intruder sent a shock of raw arousal coursing through her body. Her rigid nipples throbbed from the charge of explicit excitement. The inner muscles of her sex clenched and convulsed with hungry anticipation. Struggling to appear as stoic as the stranger looming in the shadows, Carol tried not to show any symptoms of the tingling tension that held her in its thrall. But when she released her breath and heard it drawl from her lips with a lusty and desperate growl, she knew the excitement was a secret she couldn't hope to contain.

The first spirit had revealed a montage of past Christmases. The morning when she received a pair of cuffs and a butt plug and had to use them as soon as they were unwrapped; the Christmas where she had been bound in decorative ribbons like a seasonal gift; the holiday week she had spent as a tree, unclothed and adorned with dangling ornaments and fairy lights; the festive meal where she had taken the roast's place on the centre of the table: kneeling, naked, tied, and basted. There had been a welter of punishing memories, each one strong enough to induce another degree of fetid perspiration. And Carol had understood this was the way things had always been. It was the way she had always wanted.

The second ghost had shown a series of tableaux that represented the current season. She had giggled when he described himself as the Ghost of Christmas Present. It was like the lamest pun in the world. Christmas present (here, now, today). Christmas present (gift, souvenir, token of affection). She had still been chuckling as the spirit showed her the party going on in the room beneath hers. Naked bodies carpeted the floor. Two blondes, both women she called friends, knelt in front of her master. He barked curt instructions at them as they lapped and licked at the purple flesh of his engorged cock. Occasionally, their tongues would touch as they chased their mouths against his hardness. Slyly, the pair tried touching each other rather than paying proper attention to her master's rigid shaft. Caresses slipped against bare breasts. Warm hands stroked soft, feminine flesh. Exploratory fingers dipped into wet, inviting folds. Around them was a barrage of torrid excess and cruel humiliation. Whips kissed buttocks. Candle wax dripped onto crimson skin. Clamps and cuffs bit viciously against whimpering, willing victims.

Thick shafts.

Wet holes.

Greedy moans.

Desperate pleas.

A perfume of sexual musk and perspiration seasoned each breath like the tang of mulled wine. The cruelty was intolerable throughout the room. But nowhere was it more severe than in her own torment: chained to a bed away from the party and unable to participate in the delicious and decadent depravity.

Carol hadn't been able to suppress a moan.

The Ghost of Christmas Present had regarded her with pitying sympathy. Taking her sigh as an indicator to end the series of tableaux, he snapped his fingers and showed her another element of the current Christmas.

The second scene was far less lurid than its predecessor. Carol instantly recognized Tim, her line manager from the office. He was the man who had welcomed everyone to the staff Christmas party with a reading from Matthew. It was a dull passage that he ended with a sanctimonious smile and the declaration, "God bless us! Every one." His fingers had still been wet from turning the pages of the Bible when he urged Carol into a roomy stationery cabinet and tried to force his tongue down her throat. She might have considered making his Christmas, giving in to his suggestions, taking receipt of the present he so desperately wanted to give her. But when her fingers found the meager length in his pants, she thought the breach of office protocol was not worth the effort for anything that "Tiny Tim" could provide.

Tiny Tim was shown alone in front of a Spartan tree. He stared reverentially up at the angel on its top: an angel with a face that Carol thought resembled her own. The simplicity of the scene was touching, although she felt it would have been more wholesome if Tiny Tim hadn't been fumbling with his skinny one and a half inches as he admired the angel.

And then the second spirit, and its visions, had disappeared.

She had been left to face the Ghost of Christmas Yet To Come.

"You are about to show me shadows of the things that have not happened but will happen in the time before us," she pursued. "Is that so, Spirit?"

Nothing.

Only strong-and-silent silence.

The inner muscles of her sex trembled. Her nipples ached from her need to have them touched, caressed, stroked, sucked, and nibbled. She drew a faltering breath and realized her body was already teetering on the brink of another climax. Her thighs felt sticky from the pleasures she had so far endured with all these voyeuristic treats. Her heart raced as she realized the next orgasm was building and swelling furiously in her loins.

And then the first of the visions struck her.

She was alone with a stranger. Her hands were bound behind her back. Tied with rope. The weave of the hemp scratching at her wrists. In the corner of the room an unwatched TV set showed some Dickensian melodrama with a festive theme. Her lips were wet with precome. The flavor of cock lingered at the back of her throat, as rich and cloying as the most potent brandy sauce. The dribble from her lower lip showed it was equally white and creamy. But the stranger had snatched his length from her lips. Now she was being pushed over a table and taken from behind. His shaft plundered her sex. Pushed deep into her hole. Battered her with coarse and continuous sensations.

Even though she was only watching, Carol could feel the mounting climax swell inside her body. She held her breath, sure the roaring orgasm was about to be released in a grateful and gratuitous scream.

The spirit snapped his fingers.

The vision disappeared.

Replaced by another.

On an unconscious level she understood she was seeing another Christmas. A Christmas later than the last one. She stood in a gloomy dungeon, surrounded only by stone walls. Lit by a single candle. The only thing to suggest this might be Christmas was the sprig of mistletoe suspended over the aged wooden door.

"This is to be your new home."

The voice came from outside the room. She didn't know who had spoken, but she recognized the words had come from someone powerful and taciturn. Someone strong and silent. The muscles of her sex quivered with a quiet spasm of arousal.

"This is to be your new home. Merry Christmas."

The vision disappeared as though the candle had been blown out.

The next showed another Christmas. The mistletoe over the cell door had been replaced by a stocking. It hung limp and empty from its nail. Carol was laid on the floor of the dungeon with four nubile blondes holding her wrists and ankles. Between her legs a shaven-headed master paid scrupulous attention to her sex. She couldn't fully understand what he was doing until he moved back and revealed the piercings he had slipped into her labia. The stainless steel rings glittered like the season's traditional silver bells. They looked so perfect against the flushed flesh of her pussy lips she was struck by a tear of overwhelming delight. Her master lowered his face to her freshly decorated sex and pressed a gentle kiss against her clit. As the climax thundered through her, Carol heard him whisper, "Merry Christmas."

Then the vision had disappeared and Carol saw another year had passed. The stocking over the dungeon door had been replaced by a decorative star. The rings that pierced her pussy lips were an identical match to those that dangled from her nipples.

Another vision.

Chains dangled from her piercings.

Heavy. Round. Fat. Weighty chains.

And another.

She was suspended from the stone wall, writhing in an agony of frustration and satisfaction. Sweat speckled her brow. The tops of her thighs were daubed with a viscous smear of wetness that was fresh and close to bubbling with its own passionate heat. The chains that dangled from her body quivered in a tempo that matched the echo of her own recent climax.

Another vision.

Another Christmas.

Her master stood before her with a huge slab of stone. He had cuffed her wrists behind her back. A spreader bar at her ankles made every step uncomfortable. Unbearable. The chains that dangled from her nipples and labia had been collected so they were joined with a single ring of steel. And, as she watched, the ring of steel was being soldered to the ring of steel fixed into the stone. Bright blue sparks danced from the heated tip where the links were connected.

The menacing darkness of the future vision was powerful. Carol had dabbled with BDSM before, but she had never expected to find herself being chained, pierced, and secured to stones. The totality of commitment—the dedicated involvement to submissive satisfaction—was more than she had ever thought she would find. More than she had ever dared hope she would find.

Another spasm of euphoria exploded from between her legs.

When she finally blinked the tears of satisfaction from her eyes, she realized the spirit was pointing at the vision's stone. He didn't speak. He was strong and silent and incapable of speech. He simply continued to point, quietly instructing her to obey his command and look at the stone.

"Before I draw nearer to that stone to which you point," said Carol, "answer me one question: Are these the shadows of the things that will be, or are they shadows of things that may be, only?"

The spirit remained still and silent.

The inner muscles of Carol's sex convulsed in a greedy triumph.

A shockwave of pleasure buffeted her frame and threw her into a glorious furor of release. Her body was stretched taut against the bondage at her wrists and ankles. Involuntary contractions in her abdomen pulled her repeatedly against them. And as the agony pounded through her, the flavor of the climax deepened in intensity. Staring up through a haze of red mist, Carol saw the spirit was still immovable. Understanding came like a revelation, and she instantly realized the choice she was being given.

She could continue with her current ways, subordinate to a master, enduring the punishments and penalties of being a sexual submissive. She could continue to be the bound and humiliated pain slut of her darkest and most dire fantasies. Or she could change her ways and step away from the physical pleasures of her BDSM lifestyle. She could marry and live a life of sexual frustration and pious respectability with the aptly named Tiny Tim.

Her hesitation lasted less than a heartbeat.

The choice was the most blatant no-brainer she had ever come across. Who the hell needed Tiny Tim when there were future pleasures like the stone to look forward to? The days would be hard. And every pleasure would be an absolute agony. But weren't those the best sorts of pleasures? She laughed giddily and allowed another rush of glorious satisfaction to quiver through her frame. She had been blessed with a glimpse of a bleak and agonizing future and she couldn't wait to experience every one of the painful torments she had been shown.

"God bless us," she thought cheerfully. "God bless us. Every one!"

Nog
Joel A. Nichols

On the first day of Christmas vacation, Matt drove to his parents' house for the first time in a semester, for the first time since he'd left for college—for the first time since he'd come out over the phone to his mother after Thanksgiving. Matt was listening to a holiday CD mix a friend had made for his ride home, and he sang along with Britney Spears's "Under the Christmas Tree." His friend Rider was on the road headed toward their small Vermont town from his college in Boston; he called Matt every time he passed a hot guy on the interstate.

Matt didn't have a hands-free set, so as he held the tiny phone up to his ear, he tried to stay in the right lane. They hadn't talked in a few weeks.

"Are they going to make you go to church?" Rider asked.

"Probably. They always have."

"But now you're a gay. The gay. Are they going to make you confess or something?" Matt came up on a slow-moving station wagon and anxiously swerved into the left lane to overtake it. "Hello? Are you there?"

"Yes. I was passing a car."

"Good. So didn't your mom tell the priest?"

"I don't know. Probably."

"Whatever, Matt. Don't go. They'll kidnap you or prick you with a testosterone needle—make you fuck a girl."

"Shut up." The next song was Judy, "Have Yourself a Merry Little Christmas." Then Matt said, "Whatever. They're Catholic, not evangelicals. And I've fucked girls... Look, there's traffic. I'll see you in a few hours."

Matt looked at himself in the rearview window. When you're alone in a car and you make such close eye contact, you can't lie. And he didn't mind the way he looked, up close. His eyes were brown-red and sparkled, and he liked the way the skin around his eyes crinkled when he caught himself smiling at his own reflection.

"I won't go to church," he thought to himself. "I won't let them take me."

Hours later, he pulled into his parents' snowy driveway. His legs were stiff. Matt pulled his giant duffle bag from the truck and dragged it to the front door. There were patches of grainy ice under the matted snow, and twice he almost lost his balance. He pushed open the front door. His mother stood, blocking the doorway. She hugged him hello and told him to take off his shoes.

"Your father will be back in a few minutes. Why don't you bring that thing to your room? Fill a laundry basket, and I'll wash a load before we go caroling."

He started to walk toward the staircase, dragging a snail sheen of moisture across the linoleum. Then he turned around. "I'm not going, Mom."

"But you've always gone caroling! You know we're bringing the carolers back here for cider and cookies. What are you going to tell them when they ask why you weren't out with us?"

Later, his father came home, and he heard them arguing. Their voices radiated up through the metal grates with the heat. His mother wanted to make him come caroling. But his father echoed what Matt had said to her: it was his decision. "I'll make sure he sticks around for the refreshments, though, don't worry. I want him to talk to Mr. and Mrs. Grunau and to Father Ted."

The Grunaus were old Germans whose son had died of AIDS. He was years older than Matt, but Matt remembered his solos at Mass and his starring roles in the school musicals.

He knew that talking to the Grunaus about AIDS would not prevent him from wanting to rub his cheek along a stubbly chin or cure him of falling in love with his roommate, who played ice hockey and left stinking gear in the corner of their room.

Matt came downstairs just as his mother was buttoning up her coat. His father had gone out to start the car in the frigid, snowless night. He came back in and stamped his feet. "Please warm up the cider at eight thirty. We'll be back with a crowd by nine."

"And put the eggnog out on the table, and uncover those platters of cookies. I want everything ready when we get back." She waited for Matt to nod. "It's really the least you can do, Matt, if you're not going to come with us."

He nodded again. "Rider's coming over. Is that okay?"

His father frowned. "I don't think he's the best influence for you right now."

"He's my friend, Dad. And I haven't seen him since September."

His mother rubbed her fingernail along the underside of her eyelid, searching for a mascara clump she could feel when she blinked. "We wouldn't exactly want you here with a girl alone, Matt, if you weren't, if—"

Matt blushed. "It's not like that. I don't like Rider that way. That's ridiculous! A few months ago you let him spend the night here!"

"It's not appropriate for you two to be here alone. And stop talking back. You're making us late." His mother pulled the door shut behind them, and a few seconds later, Matt watched their red tail lights disappear into the road. He dialed Rider's number and told him to hurry over.

The moon had been up for hours and it shone bright on the snow in Matt's front yard. He and Rider sat on the deck, bundled in parkas and toques, with cigarettes pinched in the *V*s of their gloved fingers. The only light came from twinkling green-and-red rope lights strung along the eaves. In long shadows, they sat next to each other on the bench and blew clouds of smoke into the cold night. Matt kept coughing.

"I can't even tell when it's smoke and when it's just my breath," he said. The smoke and icy air made his chest ache, but he accepted the second and third cigarette from Rider. "You smoke too much," Matt said.

"We live in the woods. What the hell else is there to do?" Rider stubbed out his butt on a plank of the deck and chucked it out into the snow. "Come on, let's help Peggy get her party on."

The shrugged off their coats and left them outside the door, to air out. Rider wasn't supposed to be there, so he couldn't blame the lingering smoke on him if his parents did smell it. He hoped one or two of his parents' guests were smokers so he'd be beyond suspicion. Father Ted smoked. Maybe the Foleys. Not the Grunaus.

The boys set out the cookie trays and pulled off the double layer of plastic wrap. Rider lit two red votives Matt's mother had in green glasses on the table, and Matt hefted the heavy punch bowl out of the china cabinet and set it on the table. The kitchen was dim except for the votives and plastic candle lights Peggy had perched on the windowsills.

Rider was standing in front of the fridge, with the door open, hunting for the cartons of eggnog. The fridge was full of bags of chocolate candy, coffee cans full of Chex mix, packages of butter, and four dozen eggs. "So have you gotten laid yet?"

Matt blushed. He opened the liquor cabinet and grabbed the rum. Rider saw his cheeks and said, "Come on. Don't be shy with me."

"No, not really."

"Not really? I have. I met a guy online and drove to his house."

"Weren't you afraid he might be crazy?"

"Nah. He was a little crazy. But in a good way. He let me fuck him."

"The first time you met him? Did you see him again?"

Rider shook his head. "It was good, for a first time. I came in like five minutes, though, and then we did it again."

"I can't imagine," Matt said. But fucking around was all he

had been imagining. He lay awake at night with a rock-hard dick listening for his roommate's bed to creak, staying up so late that he eventually imagined he heard it creaking. He'd peer through the shadows, trying to make out his roommate prone on the other narrow bed, to see if he could see his hands or a bulge below his waist. "I've seen some hot guys in the locker room, though. Lots of 'em."

Rider put the cartons down on the table. "I noticed you looked bigger. But what good is just looking?"

"You'd be surprised. There was this one guy...the showers in the gym have these dividers that block you from the neck up—from the neck up only. One day I was in there, and this dude was in the shower across from me. It was like a fucking beer bottle, bobbing there while he soaped up and rinsed off. Like bigger than anything I've ever seen online. And thick, too." Matt opened up the carton and the eggnog glug-glugged into the punch bowl. Rider twisted the top off the rum, but Matt stopped him. "My dad'll get mad if I put it in. But we can have a little. Grab cups."

"Did you get hard?"

Matt was looking at the rum but off into space. "What? Oh, um, yeah. I guess."

Rider poured them a shot each and downed his. "You guess? You really need to get some, Matty. Why are you being so shy? You should have shown that guy your dick. You never know—you might have gotten a little action."

"I can't." He swallowed some of his rum. "I mean, I want to. But I can't just go online. If my parents ever found out... I mean, Rider, they didn't even want you over here tonight."

"Fuck 'em. For real. All summer long Peggy and David were nice as pie to me. Then you tell them you're a homo and that I'm a homo, and now I can't even be over here?"

Rider poured himself another slug and topped off.

"They think we're gonna fuck around. And they don't want me having gay sex in their house, I guess." He finished his cup.

"What time will they be home?"

Matt looked over at the digital clock on the stove. "In an hour or so. You should leave soon—I think they'll calm down in a day or two. They were mad because I didn't want to go to church. I'm sure if I whine enough, they won't mind us hanging out this month."

The boys sat there and drank another cup of rum each. Matt filled them back up and held the bottle under the tap for a few seconds so his parents wouldn't notice any missing. He was going to have to brush his teeth.

"So that guy you had sex with. What did he look like?"

"Brown hair. He was wearing a baseball cap the whole time, so I couldn't really see his eyes. He answered the door in a fucking jockstrap. I don't remember much after that." Rider's lips were curved up in a sly smile, and his eyes looked slack, showing the drink.

Matt felt his foreskin pulling tight as his cockhead responded to Rider's description. The jockstrap reminded him of his roommate, of the stinking pile of hockey gear. He adjusted his package and crossed his legs.

"He had a hairy ass, too. But in a good way." Rider closed his eyes. "I'd love to get a piece of that right now. This is gonna be one horny month."

Matt thought about the clock, and the caroling. How he'd have to talk to Father Ted when the old priest wasn't leching on Peggy. He remembered how Father Ted had tried to talk him into the priesthood when he was fifteen. "Fuck it," he thought. "It doesn't have to be."

Rider tipped up his cup again. He arched his eyebrow.

Matt uncrossed his legs and leaned back in his chair. "Fuck them. I'm gonna jack off in the eggnog." He tugged at the fly of his pants. "Will you help me?"

Rider stood up. The front of his pants tented out, with a rock-hard circle of cockhead pointing down and to the left. When Matt saw his bulge, his dick popped through the fly of his boxers. The tip was crushed painfully against his zipper. He stood up and undid his fly. His and Rider's boners flashed out at the same time, and Matt felt his cheeks burning. He'd never seen Rider naked and was surprised at how long and thin his dick was, like a curved pencil. Matt pushed his pants down so his waistband hung loose at the bottom of his hips and his balls tensed in the air. He grabbed them with his left hand and started rubbing his glans with his right. Rider spat in his hand and cradled his cock between his palms. He stared at Matt's dick. His hungry eyes jumped from his own pumping fist to his buddy's.

Matt had leaked precome, and his cock slipped in and out of his hand with a wet snapping sound. He was still tugging, now one of his swollen balls, now the other. His brow was furrowed and his gaze focused on the punch bowl of eggnog. Occasionally, he looked over at Rider's furious jerking. The head of Matt's cock felt like silk and was bright red in the flickering light. He closed his eyes as the wave of his orgasm broke. He aimed his cock at the punch bowl and shot into the liquid. Rider took a sharp breath and grunted.

"I'm coming," he said almost under his breath and pumped a translucent pearly load in on top of Matt's. Matt, his cock listing sideways and going soft, caught his breath. He reached for the ladle and gave the bowl a stir. Rider giggled. "I better shove off. Call me, when they all go home."

A few hours later, Judy's "Have Yourself" was playing again, this time on a CD the Grunaus had brought as a present for Matt's parents. Matt was stuck in the corner talking to Father Ted, sipping a Coke. His father had topped him off with a shot of rum and a finger in front of his lips, saying, "Don't tell your mother." Father Ted was asking him about the Catholic youth group on campus.

Matt held up his hand. "Looks like you're all out, Father. Can I get you some more eggnog?"

"Thank you," he said and handed Matt his glass.

Jingle All the Way
Michelle Houston

"Purchase jingle bells, mistletoe, and red ribbons. Check. Change the sheets and make the bed. Check. Take a nice long bath with lots of bubbles. Check. Change into outfit. Check." Selene crossed off the second-to-last item. Now, all she had to do was turn on the music and she was done.

Humming "White Christmas," she tossed the list in the trash and crossed the room to the dresser where the CD player sat silent. She had no sooner turned it on than the front door opened.

"Selene? Honey, where are you?" Devin called out. Selene could hear him flicking the light switch, but since she had removed the bulbs earlier, she knew it wasn't going to do him much good.

"In the bedroom," she called back, giving a little shimmy to settle her nightgown. The tingling of bells accompanied her movements.

"What happened to all the lights?"

She could hear her husband moving down the hall, the soles of his shoes loud on the hardwood floor. Luckily, the Christmas tree in the living room, with its twinkling lights, would provide enough light for him to make his way safely down the hall.

Casting one last glance about the room, from the great soft sheets to the flicker of candlelight against the walls, she made sure everything was perfect. "I unscrewed them."

As his steps brought him closer, she reached down and picked up the velvet robe she had bought him for Valentine's Day, which he hadn't worn since.

"Why on earth did you…?" his voice trailed off as he entered the room and saw her standing there.

She swayed her hips slightly as she walked across the room, giving just enough jiggle to get her breasts bouncing and her bells jingling. "Welcome home, baby. Merry Christmas."

After setting his robe at her feet, she gave him a quick kiss and started removing his scrubs. The shirt clung to his skin, moist with sweat, but she gave a not so gentle tug and succeeded in pulling it over his head. She had just started to undo the tie at his waist when he shook himself out of his stupor. "Selene, baby, let me do that. I'm all sweaty…"

Despite his hands covering hers, she continued fidgeting with his drawstring until it came undone. After pushing his pants and boxers down his hips, she sank to her knees in front of him, the trim of her nightie brushing her upper thighs.

Devin dutifully stepped out of his pants as she tugged on first one leg then the other. Tossing his clothing aside, she leaned forward and nuzzled against his stomach, rubbing her face against the faint trail of hair leading down to his groin. "I missed you, baby," she said, placing tiny kisses along his abs.

"Next year, tell them you're not working Christmas Eve."

"Honey, you know I would have loved to have been here."

"I know." Nipping at his stomach, she stifled a grin at his surprised yelp. "But I'm glad you're here now."

Without any warning, she shifted down, taking his cock into her mouth. Sucking at his soft flesh, she slowly worked up and down his length while his hands fisted in her still damp hair. Just as he grew hard in her mouth, she pulled back and sat on her heels. "Go take a quick shower. I'll be waiting."

"Tease."

"Not a tease, but a taste of what's to come." She handed him his robe and held out her hand. After he had pulled her to her feet, she turned and crossed to the bed, the bells on her outfit jingling with each step.

"Now hurry up."

As soon as the bathroom door closed, she quickly tied precut strips of red ribbon to each of the four bedposts, working carefully to make sure each was tight. When the last one was done, she climbed on to the bed. Reclining against the pillows, she crossed her ankles and waited.

Moments later, Devin came back out, his robe on and belted, toweling his hair dry.

"Baby, you look so sexy." The husky tone to Devin's voice made her heart race. Selene patted the bed next to her. She almost couldn't breathe, she was so excited about her plans.

Devin climbed on the bed and settled next to her, leaning down for a kiss. Gently, she guided him onto his back and leaned over him.

Clasping one of his hands in hers, she pulled his arm up over his head, his wrist pressed against the bedpost. Quickly, she tied a loose knot on the ribbon, binding him. She repeated the process, and then turned around and started tying one of his feet. Her ass was bare but for the string between her cheeks, and Devin groaned at the sight.

"Why don't you scoot that luscious ass of yours back about a foot?"

Selene leaned to the side and tipped her head so that Devin could see her face. Pursing her lips, she blew him a kiss, then returned to the task of tying his other ankle to the bed's remaining post.

Task done, she slid off the bed and stood beside him, admiring her husband, tied spread-eagle on the bed. "Comfortable?" she asked.

"Except for the fact that right before my shower, some little vixen sucked my cock hard, then stopped." Selene trailed her gaze down her husband's velvet-clad body to the tent his cock made.

Selene reached out and untied the belt of the robe, then slipped the flaps to the side, freeing his cock from the weight of the velvet. Teasing him just a bit, she ran her fingertips lightly up and down the length, circling around the head, then back down to his balls. Cupping the weight in her palm, she rolled them gently in her hand as Devin arched his hips.

"Have you been a good boy this year?"

Devin rolled his eyes at her, then answered, "Yes, ma'am. But my wife hasn't. She's a bit of a tease!" He raised his voice slightly on the last word. Selene wasn't sure if it was on purpose or because she had slipped her fingertip into his ass, but if she had to guess, she'd say it was because of her.

"Your wife sounds like a naughty girl." As she spoke, Selene climbed onto the bed and straddled Devin's chest, the fur trim of her nightgown brushing against his chin.

"Oh, ma'am, she is. She's such a naughty girl, but I love her."

"Would you like to open one of your presents now, since you're such a good boy?"

Devin's eyes twinkled. "Definitely."

Selene lifted the edge of her nightgown, showing off her red-and-white lace thong with ties at the hips. Shifting forward, she lifted up on her knees and dangled one of the ties against his lips. Devin understood what she wanted. Tipping his head to the side, he caught the tie in his teeth and pulled.

As soon as he let go, Selene shifted and they repeated the process. The moment Devin let the other tie go, the thong parted and fell to his chest. His eyes widened as his gaze locked on her pussy.

She knew he was staring at the tiny red ribbons that dangled from her pussylips and ass, and the third one that was tied around her clit. "Guess where I hid the jingle bells?" she murmured. If possible, his eyes widened farther as a truly wicked grin lit up his face.

"Inside one of my presents?"

"Definitely. But first, you have another one to unwrap."

Careful not to press too hard on his shoulders, she slid forward, positioning her pussy a breath away from his lips. As his tongue moistened his lips, he inadvertently teased her already throbbing clit.

Moaning softly, she ground down on his mouth, pressing his warm, wet tongue against her needy flesh. He dived in, swirling his tongue around her pulsing clit, sucking the tiny bud into his mouth.

"Quit teasing," she panted, "and open your present."

Luckily for her sanity, he did, catching one end of the bow in his teeth. Selene lifted slightly, whimpering at the pleasure-pain as the ribbon tightened around her clit before releasing.

Reaching down, she stroked her fingers around her clit. Devin's gaze followed her every movement as right before his eyes juices dripped from her.

Thighs glistening, she leaned forward, brushing the ribbon that dangled from her pussy against his lips. Nipping the ribbon, he caught hold and Selene pulled back slowly. The first bell slipped past her lips with a muted pop, the ribbon soaked with her essence. Trembling slightly, she kept shifting back as another bell and another slipped free. She had gotten the idea from the anal beads she and Devin played with all the time, and it had taken almost a week of trial and error to find jingle bells just the right size.

As the eleventh bell slipped free, she pinched her clit and kept moving back, her inner muscles clenching tight. Selene knew the last one would send her over the edge. Breath held, she drifted back, the last bell, by far the largest, pulling against the inside of her lips. Whimpering, she dropped backward, her knees bent, and the last bell slipped free, bringing her orgasm crashing down on her. She rode the waves, prolonging her enjoyment, while Devin whispered to her. He might have been saying something important, but she couldn't tell; there was a dull roar in her ears.

Once reason returned, she sat up. Devin met her gaze, a grin on his face. "Feeling better, babe?"

"Mmm, yeah." She knew she sounded dopey, but she felt so good. Because of Devin's hectic schedule, the two hadn't enjoyed more than the most passing of intimate moments in about six months. She also hadn't masturbated in the last three weeks, in anticipation of Christmas. She wasn't certain how she was going to survive the rest of his residency, but she wasn't going to dwell on it now.

Wiggling slightly, she set the bells on her outfit to jingling again as she shifted around, until her pussy pressed against his cock.

"I do have to admit, that was erotic as hell," he said, his voice strained as she reached between them and slipped his cockhead past her pussy lips. She slid down as he lifted his hips, thrusting his cock up and into her core.

Once they'd settled into a slow and steady rhythm, Selene reached up and untied the top of her nightgown, letting the halter strap slip down, baring her breasts. She had also tied tiny red ribbons through her nipple rings. With one ribbon attached to both rings and another joined with it at its middle, it formed a festive Y, with a bell at the end.

She pushed the nightgown farther down so that it bunched at her waist even while she continued to grind against her husband. "Want to play with your last present?"

Devin nodded.

Careful not to pull too tight, Selene caught the ribbon as it dangled between her breasts and pressed the bell on the end against Devin's lips. He pursed them lightly, holding the bell between them without trapping it.

Selene leaned back slightly, her breasts jiggling as she started to rock harder against him. The ribbon stretched taunt, pulling on her nipple rings.

Whimpering as the pain sent sparks of pleasure throughout her body, Selene clenched her pussy tight, milking Devin's cock as she worked up and down, pushing them closer to a shared orgasm.

With each thrust, Devin tipped his head back, giving a tiny pull to the ribbon. Selene couldn't have planned it better. Her nipples stretched and tingled with each tiny tug. She could feel the familiar twitching of her core, heralding what was to come. Reaching a hand behind her, she gripped the last remaining ribbon and gently pulled. The first bell slipped from her ass with a well-lubricated pop.

"Oh," she gasped. Leaning a bit forward, she tugged again and a second bell slipped free. "Devin, baby, more."

The bed creaked as he picked up his pace, thrusting upward as hard as his bonds would allow him. His breath matched hers—fast and hard. They were both almost gasping as they raced to the finish line.

Another tug and a third bell slipped free. Selene fought the urge to bite her lip at the familiar sting. She clenched her pussy muscles tight as she gave a not so gentle tug and the last bell strained free. Tipping back, even as the bell dropped to the bed, she took up the slack on the ribbon attached to her nipples. Screaming at the triple pleasure, she trembled as she climaxed.

Beneath her, Devin grunted, his motions tiny jerks as he joined her. Collapsing against his chest, Selene moaned softly as the hot jets of his come flooded her.

As soon as she could move again, Selene reached up and untied Devin's arms. Nuzzling against his chest, she cuddled close. His arms wrapped around her, holding her tight. "I couldn't have asked for a better Christmas present."

Snuggling even closer, Selene sighed.

"Although I do have to wonder," Devin continued, "are you planning to untie my feet any time soon?"

Grumbling good naturedly, Selene sat up and stripped off her nightgown, then attended to his remaining bonds. Devin slipped off the robe and tossed it to the other side of the bedroom.

As they settled back into each other's arms, Devin asked, "So what's planned for New Year's?"

Selene just grinned, thinking about the bag she had hidden under the kitchen sink.

Two Gifts
Michael Hemmingson

I never thought much about sex during the holidays. It was
Christmas Eve, and Erin was supposed to come by after her
show. It was closing night of a play she was in, and we were
going to meet for a few drinks and talk about our lives. I
hadn't seen her in two years; she had been in a play I had
written and directed back when I was doing theater. She
was an actress among the many local actresses in the local
theater scene. There was something between us once—the
back and forth, casually sleeping together, brief discussions
of getting together, then silence, then nothing: more collected memories of scenes that could never match.

We started emailing again. She was still single, a single
mother, working a nine-to-five office job and doing theater at night and dreaming the things all hopeful actresses
. dream of. I found myself greatly looking forward to see-

ing her. I had visions of us picking up where we'd left off, recreating some sense of hope and love, and waking up together on Christmas morning, each renewed like Ebenezer, with cheerful music playing in the background—"hark the angels sing" and all that—and her daughter, like Tiny Tim, telling us all is well, God bless.

And then everything would be okay.

But her daughter wasn't with her this Christmas; she was in some other state with her father. I knew Erin was depressed and lonely because the only person who mattered to her was away from her on this cold Christmas Eve. It was so chilly I could see my breath form smoke in my apartment and I was wearing gloves. I had presents for her and her kid—last-minute items that I went out and bought and had wrapped because I felt it was something to do, something I had to do. It made me feel good to buy these gifts and, even better, it made me feel something.

She came by after her show—she said it was a good closing night, with half the house filled, which isn't bad for a closing—and we walked down the block to a neighborhood bar.

There were maybe seven people in the bar, some playing pool, some sitting around. We both had White Russians. I got up to go to the bathroom, was gone maybe thirty seconds, and already there was a guy sitting next to her at the counter, acting like he was going to order a drink. Twenty empty seats at the counter and he sits on the one next to hers?

"Excuse me," I said.

He turned to me.

I nodded at my drink.

He looked at my drink, then me, his eyes red, angry, like

he wanted to hit me. I was ready for anything. He moved away and there was no incident.

Erin grinned. "I haven't been inside a bar in a year. I forget what it can be like."

"Has he been waiting for me to go take a piss to make his move?"

"I've been on dinner dates when my date gets up for the restroom, men sitting at other tables immediately introduce themselves with flattering words. 'Oh, I just want to say, what a nice dress...your hair is very nice, I like your shoes.'"

"Jerks."

"People are lonely everywhere," she said.

We had a second drink and left the bar. Outside, a girl in a thick jacket, with straight black hair and heavy eyeliner, asked if we had any spare change.

"No," said Erin.

I gave the girl a dollar.

"Thanks, man!" said the girl.

"I never give anyone change," Erin said.

"It's Christmas," I said.

"Yeah. Ho-ho."

Back at my apartment, she didn't want to come inside, she wanted to go home, so I tried to kiss her and she kissed me back but said softly, "Did you think something was going to happen?"

I didn't know how to answer that.

"I just wanted to drop by, say hi, have a drink," she said.

"Of course," I said.

She left. I went inside and looked at the gifts. She called from her cell. "I'm sorry about that," she said.

"It's okay."

"It's not okay."

"You could come back."

"Some things have happened," she said. "I'm just not into that right now…"

I didn't have any booze at home. I went back to the bar. There was still an hour before last call.

The girl with the black hair and thick jacket was still outside, asking for change.

"Hey," she said, "thanks for the dollar again!"

"Want a drink?"

"What?"

"Do you drink?"

"Who doesn't?"

"Are you old enough?"

She laughed. "Funny. I'm twenty-five!"

I had another White Russian, and she had a Long Island iced tea, and then we had two more. She said her name was Taylor and I didn't believe her. She said she was sleeping in her car tonight, as she had been all week. She didn't go into details and I didn't need them.

"I live a block away," I said.

"I can't give it to you for free," she said after a pause.

"I know."

"Just to get that out of the way."

Back at my apartment, I asked her how much.

"Let's see," Taylor said, rolling her eyes. She was nervous. "Okay, look, I don't really do this, so I'm not sure what the going rate is, you know, for a blow job or a fuck or if you want to stick it in my ass."

"How about everything?"

"How about a hundred?"

"Deal."

"That was easy."

"I like it when it's easy."

I got out my wallet and handed her five twenties. She rolled them up and the money disappeared in her jacket like she was a magician.

She used my shower and then met me in the bed. Her body was taut and slender from too many missed meals— that thick jacket hid how skinny she really was. Her skin was pale and goose-bumped. I held her close to me, under the blankets, until she warmed up.

We kissed.

"This is nice," she said, like she was surprised.

"Yeah."

"Condoms?"

"Plenty," I said, reaching for the nightstand drawer, where I had a dozen assorted brands.

"Always prepared," she said.

"Always hopeful," I said.

We fucked for a while, this position and that. She was responsive and moaning. While I had her on her stomach, she said softly, "Okay, now, stick it in my asshole."

"Yeah?"

"You paid for it, boy."

"Do you want that?"

"It's what I want, now," she said, her voice changing, deeper. "Now, stick it in, motherfucker, just do it."

I did and she went limp and purred.

She started to get dressed.

"Where you going?"

"A question filled with mystery and no answers," she said.

"Don't sleep in your car. You can stay here."

It was 7:00 a.m. and I woke up to a blow job. It was nice to open my eyes and see a woman with my cock in her mouth. She grabbed a condom from the nightstand and moved on top of me. "Ho-ho-ho," she said.

This time, she said she really had to go when she put her clothes on. I was going to suggest breakfast, but she looked a lot different in the morning light. She appeared scared and confused, and I knew she didn't do this much, if ever at all. I knew she felt ashamed and I wanted to tell her not to be.

I walked her to the door.

"Wait," I said.

I picked up the two wrapped presents and handed them to her.

"Happy holidays," I said.

She didn't know what to make of this. "For me?"

"Of course."

"How…"

"I just knew."

"Thank you," she said and left.

I felt ashamed, but I was glad the presents were gone.

Flirting with Santa
Rachel Kramer Bussel

I wasn't even planning on going to my company holiday
party this year—day in and day out I crunch numbers for
this small-minded office, so why should I spend my free time
pretending to be frivolous with my coworkers? And yet it's
what's expected. Dragging my feet as I do every year, I find
myself in the midst of over-baked cookies, half-warm eggnog,
and fake friendly greetings from those who barely give me
the time of day throughout the year.

I make my way over to the drinks table to look for stronger fare than eggnog, and as I do I spy Santa out of the corner
of my eye. His head is thrown back as he laughs in delight at
something my one friend at the company, Chelsea, is saying.
The thing is, I've been here for over an hour now and have
seen almost everyone I know from work. I don't know who
this Santa could be, because any guy who remotely fits his

body type I'd have noticed by now. Even though I am pretty slim, I prefer my men big and solid. Hefty, hunky teddy bears that I can hold onto when I need to, whose weight I can truly feel when they pound into me, who I can cuddle up next to on cold winter nights.

I snag another glass of champagne and wrack my brain trying to figure out which of our many employees could have shape-shifted into such a holiday hottie. Santa looks a little lonely now, tucked away in the corner, making conversation but scanning the crowd as if looking for something, or someone. I look up and meet his eyes straight on and feel a flush of pleasure run through me, the likes of which I rarely, if ever, feel at work.

I'm the first to look away—I have to be or else I may spill my drink down the front of my dress. I go seek out my comrade-in-office-arms Chelsea to see if she knows who Santa is. "I don't know, but I know why you're asking," she smirks. She's aware of most of my sexual peccadilloes and loves to tease me from the safety of her warm and cozy marriage, but I know she still gets a thrill out of my stories and adventures.

I try to kill time, making the obligatory rounds, tasting all the sweet offerings being passed around until I can stand it no longer. I inch closer toward Santa, checking out not so much the outfit, which I'm already quite familiar with—padded red velvet suit trimmed in white, fluffy beard, jaunty hat—but the body underneath it. The way he is sitting—calm and almost expectant, with perhaps a twinkle in his eye—sends goose bumps up and down my body. Normally, I'd be getting ready to go at about this time, having made the obligatory small talk, but tonight there's nothing I'd rather do than get to know Santa just a little bit better.

I drain my glass, holding it close to my lips to let every last drop of glistening liquid slide into my mouth, knowing for sure that he is watching. My tongue darts out to lick the edges of the glass, treating the champagne as if it were cotton candy, savoring every little bit, and getting my tongue ready for action. Then I stroll toward him with an aggressive, business-like stride; it's too late to pretend that I'm not interested. I march over until I'm standing right in front of him. Then my mind stops and I realize I have nothing to say, no well-thought-out opening line. How exactly do you chat up Santa Claus?

Thankfully, he sees my distress and rescues me, his crackling blue eyes boring into mine. "Ho-ho-ho, young lady, how are you this evening?" he flings at me with all the deep warmth one would expect from Santa. I'm torn between wanting to throw myself at him and wanting to sit on his lap like a demure little girl, telling him everything—and I mean everything—I want for Christmas.

He takes my hand and, like a true gentleman, raises it to his lips for a kiss. But then he takes my index finger and, gentlemanliness be damned, slides it into his mouth, his tongue tickling the pad of my finger and sending waves of warmth throughout my body. I lean my other hand on the table as I feel myself trembling. He lets go of my hand and pulls me so that I'm flush against him, my own flat stomach pressed against his belt buckle, my breasts flush against his ample chest.

I have no idea who this man is, but at this moment I don't care, I just know that I want him, and I don't care who knows. He pulls me tight and hugs me, then rocks me gently in a mating dance so seductive I know that he'll have me begging him to fuck me before the night is out. I already am, silently, as I press my fingertips into his furry red back, rocking against him and reveling in his strength. He is calm and relaxed, as if he has all the time in the world to slow dance with me, even though I can feel his erection straining through his pants.

Suddenly, he takes my hand and leads me out the back exit, down the hallway, and into an office I never even knew existed. He locks the door behind us and then presses me up against it, his hand reaching under my skirt to find me soaking wet. He shoves two fat fingers into me and I buckle against him, biting my lips so as not to scream. After that foreplay, that intense teasing, I come quick as lightning, any semblance of control or rational thought forgotten.

And then all of a sudden, I find myself sucking Santa's cock. Now, he is leaning against the door and I am on the floor, my knees pressing into the hard wooden floor as I kneel before him. His cock is large and meaty, and I can't get enough of it. He doesn't need to urge me forward, as I've already positioned myself to take him inside me to maximum capacity. I look up into his eyes, and their bold blueness sparkles back at me, and I have to look away, close my eyes, and savor the heat of his cock as it slides in and out of my mouth.

I've been so caught up in all the holiday shopping and end-of-year calculations that I've forgotten that there are truly more important things to celebrate at Christmastime, like having someone make my heart beat that much faster, having someone whose cock gives me a reason to keep on going every day. I start to rock back and forth, moving my hips in rhythm with my lips as I slide up and down his cock, delighting when I have it all the way inside me. I start to speed up, caught up in the beauty of his hardness in my mouth, when he grabs me by the hair, stopping me. He pulls me up and drags me over to the majestic chair behind the desk, plunging into it and laying me across his lap.

His hand finds its way to my ass, and even through the

layers of my leather skirt and tights I can feel the sting as he spanks me. He doesn't bother to lift my skirt even as I squirm and wiggle, wanting more contact. My juices flood my panties as I take in this deliciously forbidden sensation. It's maddening but wonderful as I wait and take every stroke.

"Do you know what I really want for Christmas, my dear? You probably don't—nobody ever asks me, they just assume that I want nothing more than to make all their dreams come true. But I have wishes, too," he exclaims, putting an extra oomph into his smacks. "I want a girl who will do my bidding, who will be there to let me tease and play with and fondle and spank and fuck whenever I want her—a pretty girl like you who is just aching to have my cock inside her. How does that sound to you?"

I can barely reply. His words have transported me to somewhere else entirely, a world where the only thing that matters is the absolutely urgent ache between my legs, where I'll say yes to anything as long as he promises to fuck me good and hard. I twist and try to nod my head silently, but he grabs my hair by the nape of my neck.

That response isn't good enough for him.

"Answer me," he commands, his fingers finally lifting up my skirt and ripping my tights, pushing against the flimsy cotton of my panties. I inhale deeply, still unable to speak. I can feel his cock pressing even more urgently against me. He lifts me up and throws me onto the desk. I feel papers and a stapler underneath me but I don't care. "So that's what you want, huh, for me to just figure out what you're thinking? Okay, then, darling, you had your chance to speak and now you'll just have to take what I'm going to give you."

He smacks me across the face, sending the most amazing chills up and down my body. I want to ask him to do it again, but it's not the kind of thing you can demand; it only really works as a surprise.

I close my eyes in ecstatic agony, and he pulls me toward the edge of the desk. He takes out his magnificent cock again, pulls aside my panties, and plunges into me. I take a peek and see Santa before me, the large, jolly, white-bearded man I think I've known all my life. But this time he is different, this time he is slamming into me with none of the gentle wisdom or holiday cheer he is known for. He is fucking me like any real man would, hard and deep, my legs up on his shoulders, his cock hitting all the right places inside me. I squeeze his cock, loving the way I can feel each and every movement, his and mine, as we lose ourselves in this most intimate of rituals. I come, shuddering, slamming my hands against the desk as I feel my orgasm wrack my entire body. He follows soon after, letting loose a flood of heat that shoots into me.

He gives me a short moment to recover, then pulls me so I'm sitting up. I'm still half-gone, but he looks fresh and ready to roll. He draws me to the window and lifts the blinds. When I look out again I see them—the impatient reindeer snorting and stamping, angrily demanding that their owner return to them. He kisses me tenderly on the cheek and gives me a sweet, sad smile.

"Until next year," he says before opening the window and climbing out, off into the night. I stumble out the door, back to the party. I will have to wait and see what's been left under my tree; I have a feeling that whichever option he chooses, naughty or nice, I'll still be getting a special present from Santa this year.

Come to think of it, I already have.

Return Policy
Tenille Brown

Catherine took a deep breath, then pushed the plastic bag across the counter. She held up one finger to the red-haired lady in glasses who started to peek inside—the shiny tag on her blouse indicated her name was Ellen—and Catherine slowly, calmly began to speak.

"Let me preface this by saying, Ellen, that I know your return policy and I will understand if at the end of this you still tell me no. But before you say anything," Catherine said softly, choosing her words carefully, "let me just explain."

Ellen cocked her head and parted her lips as if to speak, but she remained silent and leaned forward, pressing both freckled elbows down on the counter.

Catherine began. "First of all," she said, "I'm not the type to return things— gifts especially, Christmas gifts even less so. I think it's rude and borders on tacky." She tossed a mass of heavy, dark curls across her shoulder and tugged at her jacket. "Even though I'm the one who bought the thing and could stand here in front of you and tell you any old lie—that it didn't fit, that it malfunctioned, that it irritated my skin. But, you see, I'm just not that way."

Catherine ran her tongue across her thin, faintly glossed lips. "This is the way that I am, Ellen. I am a woman who only has her husband's pleasure in mind," she said. "I'm giving, never selfish. I wasn't thinking of myself at all when I tossed on that trench coat and dark sunglasses and darted into this place in the middle of a Thursday afternoon. I was thinking of him, you see, my husband Tim."

Catherine paused. She glanced over her shoulder at a young woman with her head down, browsing through a pile of fishnet pantyhose.

"Not that I think anything is wrong with this place," Catherine continued, her focus back on Ellen, who had folded her arms tightly across her chest.

"To each his own is what I always say, though, it isn't my taste, personally." Catherine sighed. "But...I am a realist and have been married nearly fifteen years and I know that twenty minutes in the sack every Wednesday and Saturday just won't do...not any longer. Not with all those things on television and DVD these days. See, over the years, I've come to realize that it takes more."

Catherine pulled the garment from the bag then. It lay in a crumpled, red and white fuzzy heap on the counter.

"So one day I made my mind up and I came in and bought this."

And Catherine couldn't be sure, but she thought she saw Ellen smile.

"It's cute, right? And you probably sold a lot of these.

Remember that lovely Christmas display you had in the window?" Catherine didn't wait for an answer. "Of course, you do. You probably helped put the display together. It may have even been your idea. You strike me as the creative and imaginative type, Ellen."

Yes, it had been a smile. Catherine was sure of it now.

"Well, when I first saw it," Catherine said, "I laughed. I actually stopped right there on the sidewalk and had a good chuckle because even the idea, to me, was so corny. And then I thought about it more, and I thought, 'Who am I to think my sex life is so good it couldn't use a little spicing up, even if it is in a cheesy little Christmas outfit from a novelty shop?' "

Ellen opened her mouth, then snapped it shut, deciding against whatever it was she was going to say.

Catherine didn't miss a beat. "The funny thing is, I don't even like red and I'm sort of against fur. But it was obviously faux, so I figured it was all right. And Tim's reaction, well, I figured it might tickle him a little if nothing else, and then, well, in the end, all we really want is for them to take the thing off us, right?" She shrugged now. "Anyway, I put it on. It was after he opened all of his other gifts, while he was busy reading instruction manuals and hooking up gadgets. I stepped into our bedroom and slipped it on. And the thing fit quite nicely, if I must say so myself. And I pulled on these black knee-high boots I had picked up down the street—and I never wear boots; they're not my style. I skipped the fishnet hose—have to draw the line somewhere, you know. But when I stepped back into the room, Tim's reaction, well, it was shocking to say the least."

Catherine stepped closer to the counter.

Her voice became a whisper.

"We didn't even make it to his parents' for Christmas

dinner. Of course, that was fine. We see too much of them, anyway, if you ask me. And I had wanted to hang around the house and work on getting the decorations down because there's nothing worse to me than riding through the neighborhood and seeing lights up after Christmas. But he wanted to…all day. I mean, this thing was like Viagra to him. I finally had to take a thirty-minute shower just to get a breather."

Ellen's face had softened. Her eyes filled with interest, her body language screamed of curiosity.

So Catherine gave her more. "I've worn lingerie for Tim before. And he usually likes what I pick out. But he had never, ever reacted like this. I'd never seen him so—" Catherine leaned forward, her eyes darting to the left and right of her. Then she whispered, "Hard." She took a breath. "And the thing about it was the Mrs. Claus suit never came off. He went under it, he went around it, he pushed it to the side. It was like it had to be in his sight, in his hands, around him in some way. But, of course, I don't know that to be true… Well, I didn't then."

Ellen leaned in, peeking from side to side at customers browsing the racks.

Catherine continued. "Tim finally got tired around five. His mom sent around some plates—we had called and told her he wasn't feeling well, you see—so we ate, watched a little television, and drifted off. I tell you, Ellen, we both slept till noon the next day. And when he woke up, he wanted more."

Ellen held up her finger and stepped to the side. "One minute…customer."

She charged a middle-aged man thirty-five dollars for two DVDs that he kept covered with his large, pale hands.

Catherine smiled politely until the man took his black plastic bag and headed out the door. Then she spoke. "Don't misunderstand me, Ellen. I had no problem with giving in to my husband's sudden burst of sexual energy. And I still wouldn't have a problem with it today, except—"

"Except?" Ellen arched her brows.

Catherine took a deep breath. "Well, it happened gradually. A few days later, I had put the Christmas things away—the tree, the lights. I took the candles out of the windows, took down the Nativity scene in the front yard. The Mrs. Claus outfit, however, I just hung in the back of the closet. I had no plans to bring it out next Christmas or anything, I think that type of thing has an expiration date, so I just put it there out of the way, you know, until I could figure what exactly to do with it."

"Okay…" Ellen said, the curiosity in her voice rapidly giving way to frustration.

"Well," Catherine said. "Tim just wouldn't leave it be. He still wanted to—use it. And, of course, I thought that was a little odd. Not to mention that some people say it's bad luck to keep Christmas things out after the holiday, but besides that…I wanted to be obliging. I wanted to give him what he needed, so we continued to use it. But the strange thing was, Ellen, I would notice the thing always pressed between us when we went to sleep after sex. Then I'd find it on the bathroom floor when I was sure I left it in the hamper. Or I'd find it tangled in the sheets when I came home from business trips. And then, one day, I caught him."

"You caught him?" Ellen asked.

"Yes, I came home early from work. I had this terrible headache. I wasn't expecting Tim to be there. He should have been at work himself."

"But he was there. He wasn't in the living room, though, not even in the bedroom. I opened the bathroom door, however, and there he was. He was standing there wearing the outfit."

Catherine ignored Ellen's smirk. "I was appalled. I couldn't believe it. I mean, I could have been anyone walking through that door—the plumber or the exterminator. And what then? What would they think?"

Ellen's brow furrowed in confusion. "Well, what did you think?"

"That he looked just as good as I did wearing it, if not better. My husband, you see, he has the cutest little ass. And he has great legs, for a man. They're not big and bulky, not like you would think. They're not even that hairy."

Catherine was biting on her fingernails now, a twinkle in her eyes, her lips turned into a half smile. "Yes, he looked quite sexy, if I must say so myself. But, Ellen, I didn't know what to do. I stood there for every bit of ten minutes, and he didn't even know I was there. All he had to do was look up in the mirror and he would have seen me standing there, but he couldn't see past his own reflection."

Ellen's interest was obvious. "And you didn't stop him?"

"Lord, no. I didn't interrupt him. Far be it from me to try and make him feel bad about it. I mean, we all have our…habits. Mine is smoking, and I guess his just happens to be…well…"

Ellen touched her freckled skin, pulled at her curly red hair, and folded her lips tight.

Catherine continued, her voice soft and low. "Anyway, Ellen, I'm sure you can sympathize with my need to dispose of this." She pushed the outfit across the counter toward her.

"So you think returning the outfit will somehow break his…habit?" Ellen picked up the garment, shook it free of wrinkles.

Catherine shrugged. "Well, I'd never seen him in any of

my other things. Sure, panties go missing here and there, and sometimes I forget exactly where I've hung my dresses. But it's this outfit, I know it is. And I know it's safe to return it now. It's out of season and out of stock, and there will be no special order. And since it's been…worn, you'll have no other choice than to get rid of it, right?"

Catherine didn't wait for an answer.

She said, "Look, Ellen, I understand if you don't want to give me a refund. I understand if you don't want to give me store credit. But you must, you simply must take it back. Either you take it back or…"

"Or?"

"Or there will be many more days, many more nights when I walk in and he's wearing it. And you can just imagine what it's doing to me." Catherine's pulse quickened, her face flushed. She placed a shaky hand to her chest and blinked her eyes. "Seeing him there like that, all dressed up."

"Yes, ma'am, I can imagine." Ellen's skin was equally as flushed. She pulled her sweater tight over her chest, doing nothing to conceal her hardened nipples.

"And we can't have that, now, can we?" Catherine narrowed her eyes.

"No, ma'am, we can't," Ellen said. "But you do realize that our return policy is ten days and it's been nearly a month since you made this purchase?"

"I realize that," said Catherine, "and I do respect your policy, but, Ellen, I believe you can work with me in some way…" She pulled a glossy Polaroid from her purse and pushed it across the counter. "Can't you?"

For the first time within that hour, Catherine was nervous. What if she had been mistaken, had pegged the woman completely wrong?

Ellen glanced down at the picture, bit down on her lip, and pulled the bag to her. She pushed the wrinkled contents back inside and placed it under the counter.

"Consider your purchase returned," she said. "But before you go." She nodded behind her toward a display in the center of the store. A curvy mannequin wore a lacy nightie with red satin garters and fishnet stockings. "Could I interest you in our Valentine's Day special? We have it in red, since that seems to be your, um, color, and it photographs well. And if for some reason you would need to return it, say for another of our seasonal items," Ellen glanced toward the picture on the counter, "I'm sure we could work out some sort of trade."

Ellen's hands disappeared beneath the counter, beads of sweat appeared on her forehead. Catherine nodded, took the outfit one size larger than her own, and slipped out the door.

A Visit from the Man in Red
Jean Roberta

I'm not a Christian, honey, so I don't celebrate Christmas as a religious holiday. In my day, there wasn't a church that could tolerate homosexuality.

But there have always been miracles. And one of them happened at Christmastime, back before anyone I knew had heard of gay rights or women's lib. Or AIDS or global warming or crystal meth. It was a different world then.

It was 1968, and Canada's prime minister was known for being hip. He liberalized divorce and decriminalized sex between men by saying, "The state has no place in the bedrooms of the nation." The guys could still be arrested for fooling around in public spaces, including washrooms, but the government had taken a step toward sexual freedom. Lesbian sex was never officially illegal here. Most dykes I knew thought that the law hadn't caught up with us yet.

In the fall, I met Tanya in a hotel bar where hippie biker types, gay guys, and women who didn't want to meet men hung out together. Our bar drew a lot of lonely souls who had grown up like unwelcome weeds in prairie farm villages. They had all moved to the city, which happened to be the national headquarters of the Royal Canadian Mounted Police.

The Mounties didn't accept women, and their standards for male recruits were high, but that didn't prevent gay folks of all genders from imagining themselves or their tricks in the red serge jackets, the leather belts, and the tall boots.

Tanya was telling some funny story when I came in with the ex-farm girl I was dating. Tanya was the center of attention, but her soulful brown eyes flicked over us, her shiny black poodle-perm catching the light. She had healthy curves and wore a bold red shirt that set off her smooth, peach-toned complexion. She looked like trouble, yes, but she also looked like a lot of fun.

After Tanya finished talking, everyone at the table took turns telling each other their childhood dreams. "I wanted to be a cop," laughed Tanya, waving her cigarette in the air.

"Me, too," sighed a slim guy lounging beside her. "So I could hang out with them." Everyone snickered.

Someone fed the jukebox. "Wanna dance?" Tanya asked me. She seemed to have no fear of rejection. She stood up, which made her heavy breasts bounce, and I saw that she was no taller than I was, which I liked. I didn't like to be looked down on.

Ignoring my date, I followed Tanya to the dance floor where we shimmied and shook to the rock 'n' roll that was upsetting straight types all over the world. I hoped that Tanya liked me, hoped that she found my long brown hair, my girlish face, and my red stretch pants to be utterly groovy.

She cut to the chase. "Do you have to go home with the chick you came with?"

"No," I smiled. "We broke up a while ago and then got back together because we didn't want to be alone. I think she's looking for someone new."

Before closing time, Tanya bought me enough draft beer to make the rest of the evening a hazy memory. There was some yelling when I told everyone else at our table that Tanya would be driving me home, but I didn't care.

I wanted her, and I felt elated when we escaped onto the street together, running to her car like crazy teenagers. If only she wanted me as much, I thought, I would never have to regret a thing.

The next morning, I awoke in her bed. I was naked, my head was pounding, and I couldn't remember what had happened between us.

Tanya was wearing a sweatshirt and a tight, ragged pair of jeans. I thought her outfit made her look sexy and tough. Her mouth was clenched.

"Someone smashed my windshield last night," she spat out.

Fear sent a shiver up my spine. "I'm sorry," I blurted. "It was probably because of me." I couldn't believe that my ex-girlfriend was capable of such violence, but she might have had help. An impression of numerous staring eyes came back to haunt me.

"Naw, babe, it wasn't your fault," she crooned, crawling back into bed with me. "Some asshole doesn't want us to be together." She scooped me into her arms, and the touch of her sweaty hands on my breasts drove all the guilt out of my mind. She kissed each nipple like a courtly suitor, then looked at my face to see how I was reacting. "No one likes gay girls," she told me, "because we have more fun than anyone else."

"Oh, yes," I agreed.

She kissed her way down my midriff to my belly button, which she tickled until I squirmed. When she found my clit, she gently sucked it between her teeth. I grabbed her curly hair and came suddenly, mostly from nervous surprise. "Like that?" she grinned, showing me her wet face. I thought she was a sexual wizard.

I wondered if she would let me return the pleasure she had given me. I began to unbutton her shirt, and she pushed my hands away. To my delight, however, she peeled away her own clothing and threw it on the floor.

I cupped one of her generous breasts, and she laughed. When I daringly planted my mouth on her nipple and sucked, she stroked my hair. "Good girl," she told me quietly.

I wanted to turn her on like nobody else. I scratched her lightly with my fingernails so I could feel her move and hear the rhythm of her breathing speed up. She smelled like warm bread and men's cologne mixed with hairspray and cigarette smoke. I hoped I would never forget her smell.

She pushed my head downward, wanting my mouth on her. I held her hips and kissed her sweaty skin until she moaned in my ear, and then I slid down to part her thick black pubic hair and burrow into her folds to find her swelling clit. I gave it a few licks before stroking it with two fingers.

"No," she told me, trying to soften her refusal by pushing my damp hair off my face. "I don't want it like that, baby." I withdrew my exploring finger, feeling stupid. I focused on her responsive clit until she thrashed violently and gripped me in a series of spasms.

We held each other after and traded little kisses, delaying

our return to the real world, when my guilt and my hangover came rushing back.

"I'm a divorcée," I said, pressing myself against her rolling breasts. "I have a five-year-old daughter named Lisa who stays with my parents when I go out. I have to phone them."

I waited for Tanya to give me the usual sermon about the selfishness of gay mothers who refused to give their children up for adoption, even though they couldn't give them a normal upbringing. That speech never came. "If she looks like you," said Tanya, "she must be really pretty." I thought I could fall in love with this woman.

I put on my bar clothes while Tanya made toast and coffee. Over breakfast, she told me that she had been adopted as a baby and was raised as an only child. "I always wanted a family of my own," she said, as if trusting me with her deepest secret. "I'd like to settle down with the right woman and raise children. I just don't want to have babies myself."

I hoped that Lisa would like her, and vice versa.

When we were about to leave Tanya's apartment, she grabbed me from behind without warning.

I jerked. "Do you know how to fight back if someone jumps you?" she asked. Her arm was around my neck in a way that felt affectionate until she tightened her hold, putting pressure on my throat. I tried to pull her arm away, which clearly amused her.

My legs buckled, and I realized a second too late that she had kicked the backs of them with a bare foot. She helped me to land gently as I fell to my knees.

Her hands held onto my breasts as I reached around her, trying to pull myself up or pull her down with me. We ended up rolling like puppies on the carpet of her front room. "You don't know how to fight, do you, girl?" she taunted. The answer was painfully obvious. She held me down on my back, then gave me a slow, teasing kiss. I sank into an irresponsible pool of lust.

On our next date, I invited her into my attic apartment. I wanted her to meet Lisa because I really hoped, against my better judgment, that the three of us could become a family. My desire to live happily ever after with Tanya was as intense as it was hopeless. Even if the rest of the world could have accepted us, I knew that I couldn't give up all outside interests to become the wife and mother of her dreams. I couldn't do that for anyone.

I wanted to write the Great Canadian Novel, but in the meantime, I was studying to be a high school English teacher. Tanya wanted me to face reality. "You don't need a job, baby," she insisted. "If you stay home, you can write as much as you want and you won't have to worry about what anyone else thinks."

Tanya had a rare job as the only female salesperson of camping and sports gear in Eaton's department store. I thought she probably knew her inventory, but since she was paid only on commission, she could never predict how big her paycheck would be.

I couldn't trust Tanya to take care of me and Lisa. I thought I had no right to be such a burden, and I had my pride, too. In the name of common sense, I probably hurt her more than any of her tricks or bar buddies.

On a snowy winter day, Tanya tried to show Lisa how to handle a hockey stick in the parking lot behind the house where we lived. When I looked away for a moment, Tanya pretended to throw a punch at me. "It's okay, honey," I told Lisa, not wanting her to think I was being attacked.

I wanted to distract Tanya from taking me down in front of my child. "Where did you learn to fight?" I asked her.

"From a guy I knew in grade school." She smiled at her memories. "His dad was in the army. He showed me some moves after he noticed that a bunch of white kids were beating me up on the way to school. Every day. They called me a dirty Indian."

"That's bad," said Lisa. "Kids shouldn't say bad words to other kids."

I hugged her. "That's right, honey," said Tanya.

"And you're not even native," I remarked. "Are you?"

"Yeah. My birth parents were Metis. So, yeah, you could say I'm a—dirty Indian. You still wanna be my friend?" She looked angry.

"No," I sneered back. "'Cause you're not the only squaw around here. What do you think?"

I felt unreasonably hurt by her failure to sense the native blood under my own white skin. After all, she had been inside me. A lot.

"You, too?" She sounded skeptical. "Right on." She was denying her shame over what she was: not a righteous Mountie but one of the savages that the Mounties had been sent here to control, back in the time of Queen Victoria.

Tanya didn't seem to know that there was more than one way to look at history. I didn't know how to explain that to her.

Christmas that year promised to be more fun than Tanya or I had ever had before. We planned it carefully: on December 23, we would have our own Christmas at Tanya's place, complete with turkey dinner and presents for Lisa and each other.

We would cherish our memories on Christmas Eve and

Christmas Day, when Lisa and I would have to stay with my parents. I wouldn't ask them if I could invite Tanya. They wouldn't understand. She would spend those days with her bar buddies, as usual.

Our day dawned cold, clear, and snow-dazzling. "Is Tanya my auntie?" asked Lisa after I pressed the buzzer to her building.

"Sort of," I told her. "I think she'd like it if you call her auntie. But don't tell anyone else. You wouldn't want to hurt your Auntie Marg's feelings." I couldn't afford to give my snarky sister any more ammunition to use against me.

Tanya hugged us both and brought us into her basement apartment where a Christmas tree stood on a table, its colored lights brightening a dim corner like hope made visible. The smell of roasting turkey filled the space. Lisa ran to shake the wrapped presents under the tree.

"You don't get to open them until after dinner," Tanya warned her. "Be good, or Santa Claus will take them away again."

Tanya had provided a feast, including mashed potatoes, green salad, cranberry sauce, and eggnog with rum for the grownups. In the interval between the main course and mincemeat pie, Lisa sang us the carols she had learned in kindergarten, and Tanya and I joined in.

Then came the crash. The front-room window shattered in a burst of flying glass. I was so shaken that I didn't recognize the voice at first. "Fuckin' dykes! Two days before Christmas, you sick bitches! You belong in the loony bin!"

A man was staring down into the apartment from ground level, and his face was horribly familiar: Everett McLennan, my ex-husband.

Lisa was clinging to me, whimpering. She hadn't seen her

father for so long that I doubted whether she would recognize him, especially in his current mood.

"You have to pay for that, McLennan!" yelled Tanya. How could she know his name?

I felt nauseous when I heard the outer door opening and heavy footsteps approaching the door of the apartment. There would be no place to hide if he broke the door down. A cold wind from the broken window was already chilling our food and our skin, blowing my hair around my face. With ears made sensitive by fear, I heard more footsteps in the hallway, followed by a loud, incoherent argument. I could hear thick bodies slamming into each other and thudding against the wall.

Tanya was standing tensely in front of the door when a set of knuckles rapped sharply on the other side. "Police!" called a tenor voice. She peered through the peephole, then opened the door.

There stood a uniformed member of the Royal Canadian Mounted Police, a young man with a hard chest encased in red. His brown eyes were sympathetic, and his face looked surprisingly delicate. He had Everett by the arm, and Everett's wrists were in handcuffs.

"Santa Claus!" shrieked Lisa. "Don't take away my presents! I've been good! I only touched them a little bit!"

"I caught this man swinging a bat at your window," said the Mountie at the same time. "Has he done anything else to you or your property?"

Tanya stared, apparently oblivious to everyone other than our protector in red. "Officer," she said, sounding awed. "Aren't you Darryl Sangwais's friend?" Darryl was her bar buddy who had always wanted to join the police.

"I'm not the criminal here," snarled Everett. "That's my daughter and she's been exposed to immorality!"

At the time, I was so intent on convincing Lisa that the man in red wasn't Santa and that he wasn't there to retrieve presents, that I couldn't follow the conversations swirling around us. By the time I became aware of what was going on, everything seemed to be resolved.

Everett shut up and glared when he realized that Lisa was not simply going to be handed to him and that no men in white coats were going to take me or Tanya away. Once Tanya got over her first shock at meeting a gay Mountie, she told him that Everett was her co-worker and that he had been "bothering" her for weeks.

Later, Tanya explained to me that she had never told me this before because she didn't want to scare me. Our hero had been watching Everett ever since Darryl had told him that he was sabotaging Tanya at work and threatening her with worse treatment if she continued trying to brush him off. I could have told them all a few things about the devil I knew.

"This man needs to spend some time in a cell because he's been naughty," the Mountie told us, ignoring Everett's protests. "And this little girl deserves a treat because she's been good." He handed Lisa a red felt Christmas stocking that said A PRESENT FROM SAINT NICK in gold glitter. Inside, it was stuffed with chocolate bars, wrapped mints, candy canes, nuts, and a mandarin orange. "You need to get that window fixed right away," the Mountie said to us. "Keep the receipt, and he'll be ordered to pay for it." By this time, he had introduced himself to Tanya as Officer Brent Blake. We knew he was wearing his dress uniform for dramatic effect, as any gay brother would do under the circumstances.

If I hadn't known better, I would have thought Tanya was falling in love with him.

"Merry Christmas, ladies," said our gallant officer by way

of adieu. He herded Everett into a squad car, leaving the three of us, bundled up in our coats, to wait for the glazier to bring a replacement window. In the meantime, we opened presents, trying to pretend that the fresh air was raising our spirits as it reddened our cheeks.

Lisa loved the big plush panda bear that Santa had left for her earlier at Auntie Tanya's place. When I opened a little velvet-lined box from Eaton's and saw Tanya's gift of a silver ring, I hoped I could give her a discreet kiss in front of Lisa without alarming either of them.

Tanya jerked violently away from my mouth, holding me by the waist to soften the rejection. "Love you," she whispered as an explanation. We hugged for so long that Lisa wanted to join in, so we pulled her into the circle of our arms.

When Tanya opened my present, a volume of Sappho's poetry, her eyes widened. "Have you heard of Sappho, the first lesbian writer?" I asked before I could stop myself.

"No, but I'm sure she's good if you like her poems." Tanya tried to look interested. I knew that she wouldn't get past the first page.

Darkness fell early, and I needed to take Lisa to my parents' house. My flesh ached for Tanya, but we had had our day together, and we had been rescued from harm by a good man. We didn't think we could realistically ask for more.

On Christmas Eve and Christmas Day, I thought of Tanya drinking the time away with Darryl and Officer Brent. Tanya and I had agreed not to contact each other, to be on the safe side.

Lisa showed the rest of the family the stocking she had been given by Santa, who was really a policeman when it wasn't Christmas. I explained that this person was Brent Blake of the RCMP, friend of my friend Tanya. Lisa was about to tell them about her daddy and the broken window, but I asked her to sing "Silent Night" for us, instead. My parents, my brother, and my sister beamed at her, and I could almost see visions of new stepdaddies dancing in their heads.

On Boxing Day, I slipped away from my family, leaving them with a cheerful hint that I wanted to visit someone who was important to me.

Tanya grabbed me as soon as I walked into her apartment. Something had been on her mind since she had last seen me. "If you were a suspect," she growled in my ear, "you wouldn't get away from me." Both she and I could picture her swaggering in the red jacket.

Her goal was to take me down. My goal was to challenge her. As delicious as it was to be at her mercy, I wanted to prepare myself for a worst-case attack with no savior in sight. I needed to learn how to fight.

Despite being heavier, Tanya could move faster than I could. As hard as I tried to outwit her, she had me on the floor within minutes. "You better cooperate, little girl," she warned me with satisfaction.

I grabbed Tanya's breasts, since nothing else was within my reach, but this just provoked her. She pressed my shoulders and legs, holding me on the floor. She reached one hand down to unzip my pants.

"No," I laughed, trying to pretend this was all a joke. "I have rights. You can't do that."

"Can't I? Wait and see." I tried to push her off me without hurting her, and then I just tried to push her off by doing whatever seemed likely to work. Nothing did.

We struggled until we were gasping, and the outcome looked like a stalemate: I couldn't get up, but she couldn't reach my cunt without my cooperation. She managed to pinch my nipples, making them spring to attention.

She casually wrapped a hand around my vulnerable throat. "Pull your pants down, honey," she ordered sweetly. "Come on." She gradually applied more pressure until I could hardly breathe. I did what she wanted, wiggling slightly. She backed off to give me room to pull my pants all the way off.

She didn't need to tell me to spread my legs. "You're wet," she told me, calmly sinking two fingers into me. "You're gonna get it. For resisting arrest." She grinned in my face, showing teeth.

I told myself that this scenario had no connection with reality. Her tongue on my clit, however, felt very real. She sucked and nibbled it before switching to hard fingers that tormented it to an explosion. I knew from experience that this was just the introduction, with the main course to come harder. "Give in?"

"Yes." I was breathing hard. Tanya entered me with two, then three, then four fingers.

"I want to fuck your brains out," she told me in a voice that was soft but dangerously quiet. "Poor girl," she laughed. "You can't stop me, because I'm bigger than you." I could hardly hear her words when she was filling me so well.

Like a military strategist, she proceeded with cunning and persistence. She spread her fingers inside me, pressing deeper. She took my moans as a cue, responding to my most interesting reactions. Eventually, she was slamming her fingers into me, and my cunt served as an echo chamber to amplify the sweet ache of each thrust.

Afterward, we lay on her floor in each other's arms, catching our breath, thinking our own thoughts. I was surprised to feel her tears wetting my face. "I'm sorry, honey," she groaned.

"I'm a bastard to you. I don't really mean it."

I wondered whether her birth parents had ever been married. "I know," I told her, trying to hold her tightly enough to show how I felt. "Honey, it's okay. I wanted you. And we're innocent under the law. Think about that."

We both remembered the sight of our own gay Santa Claus defending us in a way that no real man ever had before. And he was twisted and queer like us, defying his superiors every day just by being himself. Tanya snickered, and we ended up rolling all over the floor, laughing in each other's faces until we both had tears in our eyes.

At length we lay quietly. She was on her back, and she held me on top of her, my head between her breasts. Not having to look me in the eyes seemed to give her courage. "We're not going to spend our lives together, are we?" she asked.

"No, woman," I answered. "But we can be friends. We'll be okay."

Even though we had lost something, we still felt saved and blessed by our Christmas miracle. We knew that some dreams could come true and that the future of people like us was worth fighting for.

Everything You Need on Christmas
Brooke Stern

Waking up in the morning, it took Laura a few groggy minutes to remember today was Christmas. Simon was breathing
softly next to her, and she curled up with him and closed her
eyes. Try as she might, though, she couldn't fall back to sleep.
She found Christmas upsetting. She was happy not to wake up
alone—that in itself made it better than most of her Christmases—and she was far from family, which dramatically cut down
on the number of things that could go wrong. Nonetheless, she
couldn't feel as carefree as she might have on other mornings.
On Christmas, the voices were louder and more persistent:
What was wrong with her? What was she doing here? Thirty
and no husband or kids. An ocean separating her from family,
and something even more insurmountable separating herself
from home. New York with Simon was okay. Better than okay,
but at that moment nothing felt very good at all.

Was it too early to drink?

"Merry Christmas," Simon said when he awoke.

They had agreed no gifts, no fuss. She would have pre-
ferred no tree, but Simon already had one up when he had
first taken her back to his apartment. She hadn't pegged him
as the Christmas-tree type. She had had plenty of time to
speculate on his type during the semester, which she spent in
the back of his Victorian novel seminar, biding her time until
after finals when he would ask her out without asking to get
fired from his job.

"Come on. I'll make you breakfast."

He had already gotten up and put on jeans and a T-shirt.
She picked up the shirt he had worn yesterday from off the
back of a chair. It almost came down to her knees and made
her feel very small.

"You all right?" he asked as he chopped scallions for an
omelet.

"Tell me a story?"

"What kind of story?"

"A Christmas story."

"You mean like Dickens?"

"No, I don't want a moral."

"An immoral Christmas story?"

"Yeah."

"The Victorians wrote a lot of immoral stories, but I don't
know if any of them were Christmas stories."

"They did?"

"Yeah, Victorians were obsessed with their porn. It was all
about incest and spanking."

"It was?"

"Yeah. Pretty wild stuff."

"Oh."

Laura lost her nerve and ate her omelet in silence. It was all about incest and spanking. She repeated his words in her head, trying to recall his tone of voice, looking for any hint as to how he felt about them. Did he see her blush? Could he detect the feeling in her core of being found out, of having her deepest secrets writ large as a nineteenth-century literary phenomena?

"You seem down," he said when they were sitting on the couch.

"It's just Christmas. I'll get over it."

"Can I get you anything?"

"You mean like presents? We said no presents."

"I mean like anything."

"Do you have any of those stories?"

"What stories?"

"Victorian stories."

"The dirty ones?"

"Yeah."

"Not here. I have some at my office."

"Do you like them?"

This was her big question and she hoped he would just answer it.

"They're pretty trashy, but..."

"But?"

"They can be kind of hot."

"Even the..."

Her words faded away but Simon—bless him—filled in the blanks.

"Even the incest and spanking?"

"Yeah."

"What will you do if I say yes?"

"You mean will I be disgusted and storm back to the women's studies collective?"

"Yeah."

"No, I won't."

"Then, yes, even the incest and spanking."

She could tell it was hard for him to say.

"Will you do it?"

That was hard for her to say.

"What?" he asked, but only because he didn't know what to say. It was his turn to feel found out.

"For me."

"Really?"

"For Christmas."

"You want everything?"

"Yeah."

He turned a corner in his head and his voice changed from apprehensive to wicked.

"You need everything, don't you?"

"I do."

"Even the naughty parts?"

Just like that, Laura was wet.

"Even the naughty parts."

"It's extra naughty on Christmas."

"That's what I want for Christmas. Make it as naughty as you can. Just like the Victorians."

As naughty as you can was pretty bold. Simon wondered if she knew what he was really capable of.

"You'll do as I say?"

"Yes."

"'Yes, Daddy,'" he corrected, filling in the final piece of the puzzle.

"Yes, Daddy."

She had to close her eyes and follow his lead on faith. It made her tremble.

"You haven't been a good girl this year, have you?"

"No, Daddy. I haven't."

"You know what that means?"

"I know you have to do it, but can you be nice to me, too? I don't think I could stand it if you were mean."

"Daddy doesn't want to be mean to his little sweetheart. He's only doing what he has to, no more, no less. He wishes it didn't have to be this way. He wishes it didn't have to hurt so much."

"But, Daddy, it's Christmas. Please don't ruin my Christmas."

"I'm so sorry, Laura. After what you've done, I'm afraid I have no choice. You'll have to be punished before any of us will feel any better, okay?"

"It'll hurt too much. Please, Daddy. What if I can't take it?"

"Bend over, Laura. That's fine. The arm of the couch will do."

"But I don't know if I can be a good girl."

"You just behave yourself during your spanking and everything else will take care of itself."

"Okay, Daddy."

"This is from Daddy, sweetheart. It's going to hurt but not because I want to hurt you. It just has to hurt so that next time you'll be good."

"I'm sorry, Daddy. Don't do it too hard. Please don't do it too hard."

"It will all feel better afterward, sweetheart. I'm sorry it has to be this way, but it does."

It was a drama that fit them both like a glove and put them right where they wanted to be. It was a script straight from one of those Victorian underground novels, but it felt as if it could have been written for them. For Laura, this exceeded her wildest expectations. She hadn't pegged him as this type, either. He had seemed so together, so not a perv, so not like her. This was the best Christmas ever, she thought, even when he had flicked up the tail of his own shirt to bare her bottom and begun spanking her hard.

Even when her backside burned and each spank was unbearable, she imagined the moment after he had finished, when she would look up at him with tear-filled eyes and ask Daddy for what she really wanted. She fled the fiery pain on her flesh and fast-forwarded to the time when he would fuck her right here, bent over the arm of the couch, and her cries of pain would change into cries of pleasure and she would exorcise all the ghosts of Christmas past. This was what she had needed. This was what she had always needed.

"Do it hard. I need you to do it hard," she said when the time finally came. She heard the distinct sounds of belt unbuckling and zipper unzipping.

"Don't worry, sweetheart. Daddy will give you everything you need on Christmas."

Christmas Blizzard
Teresa Noelle Roberts

"Another cancellation," I sighed as I hung up the phone.

The promise of a "blizzard of the new century" threatening to rival the infamous, deadly Blizzard of '78, here on the far tip of Cape Cod where snow rarely sticks at all, had cleared the few winter tourists out of Provincetown long before the snow actually hit. I'm sure some of the locals were pleased, but it was making for a less than happy holiday at our bed-and-breakfast. We'd been booked full for tonight, Christmas Eve—women who'd decided on a romantic holiday in P'town and either breakfast in bed or a big pajama-clad, family-style breakfast on Christmas morning—but one by one, they'd been canceling. The couple who'd just called had been our last holdouts; they'd gotten as far as Providence, Rhode Island, on their way from New York City, creeping through a near whiteout, and had decided to hole up in a hotel there for the holiday instead of risking the rest of the drive.

Lucie circled her arms around me from behind. "Look on the bright side. We have Christmas to ourselves! When was the last time we got to spend a holiday, any holiday, without an inn full of guests? And we can enjoy the inn all decorated and pretty instead of hiding up in our little cave." Her hands slid up from my waist to cup my breasts. "What's the point of owning a lesbian romantic haven if we can't enjoy it ourselves sometimes?"

Good point, I thought, as her small, hard hands sent waves of sensation radiating out from my breasts. Our apartment above the garage was the only part of the property we hadn't succeeded in making luxurious, the only part we hadn't bothered decorating for Christmas—solstice—generic midwinter cheer. But left alone, nothing would stop us from enjoying all the amenities we offered to guests. "Let's start in the Lavender Room," I whispered. "I'd gotten it all ready for the folks who just called."

We all but ran there. We'd had a fire going against the window-rattling gale, and the room was toasty warm, the flames casting interesting shadows on the lavender walls. We shared a quiet moment enjoying the sensation of pretending to be guests, appreciating the beautiful color scheme we'd chosen, the richness of plump pillows, velvet duvet cover, brocaded drapes. The room smelled delicious, like Christmas cookies (we'd gone crazy baking for the guests and would now be eating gingerbread women and pfeffernüsse for weeks), wood smoke, pine, and, of course, lavender. Yeah, our guests had it pretty good—and today, so did we.

Then clothes began flying everywhere. Soon we were naked and lying in each other's arms on the Oriental rug in front of the fire.

Just long, languid kisses at first, and pressing together, loving how our breasts brushed against each other, how our legs intertwined to allow maximum skin contact. The warmth transmuted into heat and the heat filled me, igniting nipple and clit and pussy and every inch of skin in between. From her movements against me, I could tell Lucie was in the same place. It had been a long time since we'd taken the time to just make out like this.

Finally, I pulled away, sat up. Lucie's skin glimmered with a fine sheen of sweat. Her nipples were hard, crinkled with excitement and moisture gleamed between her parted legs. "Beautiful," I breathed. I moved to touch her, but she shook her head. "The floor's hard, and I've always loved that sleigh bed."

If I could have picked her up and carried her, I would have. It seemed appropriate in that room with its Victorian aura. Alas for that fantasy. Lucie, while shorter than I, does chimney work in fall and winter and landscaping in summer, and she's dense with muscle. So I just gave her a hand up instead and whirled her over to the bed.

It was high and puffy and enveloping and her café-au-lait skin—Lucie is an interesting ethnic mix that includes Cape Verdean, French-Canadian, and Mohawk—looked both darker and creamier against the purple velvet duvet. I dove onto the bed next to her, squealing, "Whee!" and for a minute all we could do was giggle. Then I began to stroke her and the giggles faded into sighs.

Silken skin over firm muscles, and small breasts with prominent, plum-colored nipples, and the tight, black curls that drew my eye to her pussy, just as plum dark as her nipples and now juicier than any plum I'd ever encountered—I stroked and kissed my way down Lucie's body to that spot and began to lick.

I've given a lot of thought to what Lucie tastes like. The briny sweetness of oysters—Wellfleet oysters, eaten in Wellfleet just hours after they were harvested—always come to mind, but there's a hint of smoke and spice there, too, and a fragrance that adds to the mystery. Lucie tastes like Lucie, I suppose, and she's delicious.

She filled my mouth, my nostrils, all my senses. In turn, I filled her with two fingers, crooking them to tantalize that sensitive little node that someone unpoetically named the G-spot. Slick and smooth and gripping, she rode my hand and mouth, cooing and mewling to herself. Strangely ladylike noises, as if she were afraid of being overheard. But that was just Lucie's way. At other times, she's outspoken, with the hearty voice of someone who works outdoors a lot. In bed, she becomes deceptively quiet. (For the first year we were together, I tried everything I could think of to make her scream or at least moan when she came. Then, I decided it was just the way she was wired, and since it didn't interfere with her enjoyment, I wouldn't let it interfere with mine.) There was nothing quiet or ladylike about the way she was thrashing around, though, or the way she clenched around me.

And even less ladylike was the way she returned the pleasure once she'd caught her breath. She knows I like a little roughness sometimes, and there was something especially perverse about her pinning me down with her body weight and working me over in a lush Victorian space lavishly and sentimentally decorated for Christmas. Love bites on my breasts and fingernails raking my thighs were just the start, enough to make me wet and squirming and loudly excited.

"Onto all fours, darling," she said huskily. It wasn't an order—we're into sensation, not power play. Still, I rolled over obediently and stuck my ass into the air. Why not? I knew what was coming and I knew I'd love it.

With a thwack her hand came down on my butt. I jumped at the sudden sting, even though I was anticipating it, but heat blossomed from the impact immediately, spreading from my butt throughout my whole body. I arched my back, raising my ass to show I wanted more, and was promptly rewarded. The pleasure built as the spanking continued, spiraling from her wicked little hand through my pelvis, right into my cunt. Unlike Lucie, I'm not quiet when I get excited. Pretty soon I was yelping, growling, and occasionally giggling from the adrenaline rush.

And pretty soon after that I was begging incoherently.

"What do you want?" she demanded.

"Please…" This was not the time to ask a girl to speak in complete sentences, but if I couldn't say what I wanted, I certainly couldn't string together a concept that complex.

"Please what? Please stop spanking you?"

She said that just as I grunted out another "Please." It was poorly timed—she did stop spanking me.

That provoked one other word: "Bitch."

"Your bitch, though."

I nodded. Then I raised my ass even higher and managed to squeak out, "Please make me come."

She leaned around me, nibbling my ear in passing. "Hey, that was almost articulate. Can't have that."

Her fingers touched my clit, began to circle. With her other hand, she smacked me again, a little faster and sharper now that I was so close.

I howled as I came.

"Happy holidays," she purred. "Consider this the stocking gift—there's plenty more to follow!"

Later, as the storm hit the Cape in earnest, we headed down to Race Point, bundled in our warmest clothes. We clung to each other as we walked, partly against the force of the wind but mostly because we love to touch, even when the touch is muted through layers of fabric. The crash of the storm-fueled waves and the roar of the wind combined into a white noise that we couldn't talk over. I love the ocean when it's so wild and dramatic, but big areas of beach have been known to wash away when the seas get so rough—we lost entire buildings during the Blizzard of '78—and Lucie finally dragged me away as the snow began to fall thicker and faster.

It was flying fast by the time we got home, obscuring the Christmas lights that brightened the town and the sliver view of the harbor you can usually see from our apartment, the one saving grace of the cramped space. We stripped out of several layers of clothing (pausing frequently to smooch) and made ourselves hot chocolate (pausing frequently to cuddle up against each other and nibble).

"I'm still chilled," Lucie said after we'd finished our cocoa. "How about a hot shower together?"

That sounded like a good idea, but as I rose to take her up on it, I looked out into the yard and got a better one. Snow fell steadily and thickly against the twilight—if you could ignore the howling wind and the fact we couldn't see the house next door despite it being blanketed in a truly scary light display in the shape of an unusually buff Santa waving a Pride flag—it was an idealized Christmas Eve straight out of an old movie. The house and the privacy fence sheltered the back deck from the worst of the wind, so it was falling straight down instead of blowing sideways as it was out on the street. "Ever made love in a hot tub in the snow?" I asked.

Lucie grinned. She was already struggling back into her boots before she answered, "Not yet!"

I don't think we'd ever made it downstairs so fast. I made one detour—to turn on the outside speakers so our favorite offbeat versions of holiday classics filled the air—but that took mere seconds since the music mix was already set up.

Certainly, we'd never gotten the cover off the tub so efficiently for our guests.

We eased ourselves into the water and melted together, kissing frantically. The snow, a thick veil around the tub, was searingly cold on my skin at first, but within a few minutes the steam from the tub began to do its work, and most of the flakes evaporated before they hit us. Some lodged in our hair, cooled our shoulders and necks, but it was just enough to feel good, to remind us of the power of the storm. The windbreak wasn't complete, but as long as we stayed mostly underwater, it was all right.

More than all right. It was downright miraculous to be out here on Christmas Eve in the middle of a storm, buoyed up by hot water and surrounded by Loreena McKennitt working her strange magic on "God Rest Ye Merry Gentlemen." All the better to be so in the arms of the woman I love.

My hand slipped between Lucie's thighs, finding a slick warmth, hotter than the water surrounding us. I started to stroke, but then had an inspiration and positioned her over a low jet on her hands and knees. She arched her back in pleasure, dancing multicolored lights illuminating her expectant face and her short dark hair spangled with snow flakes. "You're evil," she gasped. "Brilliant but evil."

"Jets are a girl's best friend—I can't believe you never tried it before."

"Never had a chance. We've mostly used the tub when it was full of guests."

She was right, of course. We'd only put in the hot tub early this fall, after a successful summer gave us the spare cash. During the slower parts of the fall and early winter, we'd been busy with postseason repairs and redecorating and getting ready for first Thanksgiving and then Christmas, and collapsing in small, exhausted heaps when we weren't up to our eyebrows in some house project. And we'd gotten used to thinking of the tub as the guests' domain, not ours.

Important safety tip: take time for ourselves more often.

"Like it?"

"Oh, yes."

She was purring, but she still sounded much too coherent. I crouched over her, cupping a breast with one hand, pushing two fingers of the other inside her. So hot and tight, gripping against my hand. Slow in-and-out fucking, pushing against her swollen G-spot, my thumb on her clit and the relentless caress of the jet. She was so hot that I expected the snow to sizzle as it hit her, but it just melted, joining the water that made her body gleam. "Are you going to come for me?" I whispered in her ear, and she convulsed silently.

I didn't let up, though. Lucie, once she got going, could come for a long time. There's nothing I like better than seeing her become utterly boneless with lust, and she certainly obliged, bucking and contracting against my fingers in wave after wave of orgasm and cooing softly.

Until suddenly her noises weren't soft anymore. She bucked back against me, almost pushing me over, arched, and howled her pleasure to the snowy night, drowning out the carols, drowning out the howling wind. Drowning out everything but the roar of my blood.

The sound echoed through my clit, ringing me like Santa's sleigh bells, only much sweeter. I'd forgotten, after years with Lucie's quiet ways, how hot a screaming woman can be. (Okay, I hadn't forgotten it. I just hadn't let myself spend too much time being wistful over the one thing missing in a great relationship.) These unfamiliar—yet entirely Lucie—noïses galvanized me, pushed me toward the edge as fast as a touch might. I ground myself against Lucie's shuddering body and added my own cries to hers.

We slumped down together, boneless. Somehow, we managed to arrange ourselves so we were supported on the seat and not in danger of drowning. I can't speak for Lucie, but I know in my case brains weren't involved in the process. I pulled her close, cuddled her still-shuddering form against me.

"Wow," she choked out, and buried her face against my shoulder. A little while later she repeated it. "Wow."

"I've never heard anything that beautiful, love. What broke the dam?"

She shrugged. "I don't know. The jets. You. The contrast between hot and cold. You. This amazing storm. You. Christmas Eve magic. You."

All around us, the roof tops and holiday decorations of Provincetown were disappearing under snow. Our own deck was getting buried except right around the hot tub, and the lights on the backyard trees were obscured by snow. We'd freeze getting back to the apartment, and cleaning up once the storm was over would be backbreaking. And at some point I'd have to think about all the income we weren't getting from the canceled bookings. But for now, safe inside our private Christmas Eve of steam, hot water, and desire, that didn't matter.

"Hearing you let loose like that was the best Christmas

gift you could have possibly given me, love," I whispered to Lucie.

She giggled in a floaty way, still on a post-orgasmic high. "That's good," she said. "I didn't have much time to shop. But I think I can give that present over and over—now that I've found it."

Mulled Wine
Dominic Santi

"Why does your dick taste like mulled wine?"

If Glen and I were monogamous, that would be a problem. Fortunately, we're not. So I grinned when I looked down at him and said, "I stopped at Jake and Karl's Christmas party on the way home."

"Oh, indeed!" Glen leaned forward, once more sucking my dick into his mouth. His short blond curls bobbed against his Santa hat and his blue eyes twinkled up at me. I loved watching his cheek bulge out as my dick hardened on his hot, wet tongue. He sucked me long and slowly, like he was drawing the flavor off my skin to differentiate each of the specific tastes.

"Cinnamon, clove," he laughed, pulling back so his saliva dripped off my dickhead. "Perhaps a hint of allspice."

I shivered as he flicked his tongue down my shaft, like a

snake smelling. He paused to suck my skin into his mouth, massaging with his tongue before he worked his way back up, and swallowed me deep. He was panting when he finally came up for air.

"How's about you give me all the gory details, hot stuff, while I feast on your exceptionally delicious dick and get you naked." He once more kissed down my shaft, this time untying my shoes with one hand. "I'm in the mood for something festive."

I saw no reason to argue with the man sucking my dick. Just as I'd expected, Glen had ambushed me when I walked in the door. "Festive" barely began to describe his attire. He was naked except for the Santa hat and a shiny steel ring encircling the base of his cock and balls. A large pair of jingle bells hung from the bottom of the ring, swinging merrily on red and green curly ribbon below his freshly shaved scrotum and his upthrust cock. On one nut he'd painted Luv, on the other, U, in what I had no doubt was the spearmint-flavored, glow-in-the-dark, red body paint I'd seen him admiring when he was perusing the latest and greatest at his favorite online sex-toy store last week.

"God, I love the way you have fun," I laughed. The sound segued into a moan as he deep throated me again. He hummed the first bars of "Jingle Bells" along with the CD he had playing in the background, his voice vibrating over me until I was shaking. Then he pulled his mouth off my dripping dick and slid the first shoe off my foot.

"The wine, my love…"

I balanced my hands on his hat as he deftly peeled off my shoes and socks and disposed of the pants puddled around my ankles.

"Jake sent me an email I couldn't refuse as we were closing

up for the day. I followed him home, reminding him you and I had plans, so I couldn't stay late." I looked down meaningfully into Glen's sparkling baby blues. He slurped my dick back into his mouth, rewarding me with a sucking kiss that left me shaking. "B-by the time we got there, Karl and his buddies had a fucking orgy going on. There must have been thirty people roaming around the house, and it was barely six." I threw off my jacket and tie as Glen sat up and yanked open the buttons on my shirt. I tossed that aside as well. "Four guys in elf hats were straddling the coffee table, trying to fuck in a daisy chain to 'Santa Claus Is Coming to Town.' Fantastic hors d'oeuvres, bowls of mint-flavored condoms—and lots of mulled wine. Fuck, that feels good!"

I moaned, grabbing Glen's head as he again dove down on my dick. He was laughing so hard I was surprised he didn't choke. I fucked in and out of his mouth, panting hard. "I told Jake I was only going to play for a while, and I didn't want to come as that would interfere with our plans here. That's when he dunked my dick in his wine and told me they'd be going strong all night, if we wanted to 'come' by later." As Glen looked quizzically up at me, I locked my fingers in his hair. "Up to you, sweetie. At the moment, I'm right where I want to be." I tipped his chin up so our eyes met and held. "I wouldn't miss our holiday tradition for the world."

Nodding, he winked and went back to licking my dick. Then he licked his way up my belly and up my chest and neck until we were swallowing each other like anacondas. Still kissing me, he grabbed hold of my dick and led me into the living room.

A fire was blazing in the fireplace. The coffee table had been pushed aside. In its place was Glen's exercise mat covered with red satin sheets. A pile of holiday throw pillows on the mat glowed in the firelight. On the floor on a short wooden tray were two full crystal water goblets and a silver bowl of unwrapped candy canes. Still holding my dick, Glen led me onto the middle of the mat and pushed me down on my back. Facing me, he dropped to his knees and straddled my head, so his scrotum hovered over my mouth.

"Read your Christmas cards, hot stuff," he said, lowering himself until his painted balls were almost touching my lips and those damn jingle bells rolled forward to tickle my nose.

I could read, all right. "I love you, too," I laughed, sticking out my tongue. As my taste buds exploded with the taste of mint, Glen squatted farther down. I filled my mouth with the firm, smooth heat of his low-hanging balls. He moaned as I washed them clean, licking and sucking with the same fervor he'd shown my shaft, tangling my tongue on those damn bells and ribbons, and worrying my lips over the body-warmed metal of his cock ring. Even over the mint, I could smell sweat and soap and the scent that was so uniquely my man's.

When Glen shoved a pillow under my head, I groaned in anticipation. "I'm going to choke on these fucking bells."

"No, you won't," he laughed. He grabbed a pillow for himself and turned around. The bells jingled merrily as he again positioned himself over my chest. He squatted back, his cheeks spread wide, revealing the beautiful pink pucker aiming right for my mouth. His warm, hard cock pressed against me and those damn bells rolled back beneath my chin. I resisted the urge to lick as he leaned forward and lifted my legs, spreading them wide and bending them back under his arms. He's just enough shorter than I that we fit together perfectly. My hard-on pressed against his chest.

"Merry Christmas, love," he whispered, blowing gently. I arched up, shivering as his lips came down. Then he was kissing my hole. With a heartfelt moan, I stuck out my tongue and indulged in the long, slow lick I'd been longing for.

I felt Glen's groan in every bone in my body. His hole was beautiful, a tight little pucker. It swelled up warm and tangy and sensitive when I worried it with my tongue. As I wet him to glistening with my spit, Glen's kisses deepened. I pulled my legs farther back, opening myself wider to him as he dug in deep.

"Fuck, that feels good." I gasped as he drilled his tongue into me. Putting my fingers on either side of his spit-covered pucker, I spread his cheeks wide. He was tonguing me harder, wiggling his ass, leaning back farther as I stretched him. I licked one finger, put it in the center of his pucker, and rubbed.

Glen went wild. He rocked his chest over my hard-on, leaning back as he feverishly licked my hole.

"So good!" he panted, squirming uncontrollably as I pressed my fingertip in. As much as Glen loved sixty-nining, his concentration went all to hell when I penetrated him. He licked and sucked my hole for all he was worth, but every other thought process in his brain drained south to where my lips and fingers were. I slowly spread his sphincter, working in both index fingers up to the first knuckle as I gradually stretched him open and lapped my way into him. What he was doing to my ass was driving me nuts. Glen went wild, moaning and writhing and tongue-fucking me as the muffled bells jingled against my neck. I washed him with spit until his hole was dripping and I was shaking. Then I reached into the silver bowl.

The candy canes had been Glen's idea. He'd spent hours on the Internet, researching and later taste testing and "environmental" testing various brands until he found the perfect ones that were wide and strong and smooth enough for what he had in mind. The week before our first Christmas together, he'd seduced me into another of the mutual rim jobs we loved so much. And he'd brought out his pièce de résistance. I'd never come so hard in my life.

He moved in with me the next day. Every year since, we'd celebrated our anniversary the same way. I knew what was coming tonight. So did Glen. He groaned at the soft clink as I wet the candy cane in the water glass. I kept licking, gentling his hole open even as I spread his cheeks wide with the fingers of one hand. Then I pushed his hips slightly up, ignoring those damn bells as I touched the wet candy to his pucker. Very slowly, I twirled the tip of the cane.

His pucker clenched, quivering as I rubbed the sticky peppermint into the spit. I licked around the stick, careful not to penetrate him, my mouth tingling with the onslaught of mint. Glen panted and shook above me. When my lips were as sticky as his hole, I licked him wet again. Then I blew softly over his skin.

Glen jerked up hard, crying out as I turned the cane sideways and rubbed it back and forth. Each time I blew, he shuddered hard.

"You know what's coming next, hon," I whispered. I dunked the candy cane in the water again. Spreading him wide, I again dug my tongue in deep. He was so warm inside, so smooth on my tongue as I drilled through his trembling gate. I sucked the sides of his sphincter, savoring the flavor of his skin blending with the mint on my taste buds. This time, when I withdrew my tongue, I had the dripping candy cane waiting. I touched it to his now loose and slippery hole, and slowly, deliberately twirled it in.

Glen bucked up, yelling and clenching his ass muscles as I

gradually worked a good inch of the candy cane past his now darkly flushed and slightly swollen pucker. I took the candy out, tonguing his minty, hot hole while I dunked the cane in the water again. Then I fucked the slippery, sticky toy back into him, slowly working my way up. As his tongue flicked erratically over me, I slowly and relentlessly slid the peppermint inside him, watching the red and white stripes disappear to the two-inch "safety" line Glen had painstakingly marked on the cane.

"You like?" I growled, keeping up the long, slow fucks as I licked my minty spit up the back of his balls and over the metal ring surrounding the base of his rock-hard dick.

"Oh, God, yes!" he groaned, grinding his cock against me as I twirled the cane in and out of his ass like a barber pole. "It's hot, and it's cold, and it burns, and I love it! Fuck, I love it!"

With his whole body shaking, he jerked my legs farther up and drove his tongue into me. I've been a slut as many years as my sweetie has. At the feel of his tongue, I relaxed my hole and let him take me to heaven. His hand fumbled as he reached for his crystal glass. He swore loudly as he knocked it over. Bracing himself on one elbow, he dunked a candy cane into my water glass. Then he was between my legs again, his elbows pressing my thighs back and open as his fingers spread my asslips. I could feel the hint of heat on his fingers where he gently caressed my sphincter. In front of me, his asshole still fluttered ecstatically over the candy cane buried two full inches up his butt.

"Don't move the cane," he choked out, licking my hole as he wet me. "I need to concentrate."

Holding the handle of the candy, I left the cane buried in his ass and stilled my hand. I kissed the sticky, mint-flavored flesh in back of his balls as I braced myself for what I knew was coming. But even with all the times we'd done this, I could never really be prepared. I felt the delicious twirl and slide at the same time I felt the heat. Then I felt the cold and the burn and the vibration of Glen's laughter. I yelled and bucked up and the cane slid in its full two inches in one long glide.

I thought I'd never stop shaking. Glen fucked me until I was twitching so much I could hardly breathe. As my balls climbed my shaft, he shifted, just enough for me to suck his cock into my mouth. I tasted mint as his dick slid down my throat. I felt the burning cold, and the wet heat of his mouth closing over my shaft. Then we were a frenzy of fucking, sucking, juicy holes and dicks as we ground together and sucked each other off and fucked each other with those fucking candy canes until we sent each other into orbit with orgasms that literally had me seeing stars. My balls drained themselves dry, and I sucked his come down my throat until he collapsed on top of me. We lay there for the longest time, totally blissed out and holding each other tight, covered in sticky, minty come with the candy canes still buried up our butts. Finally, Glen lifted his head.

"That is really starting to burn," he laughed. He was still out of breath as he clenched and unclenched against the candy cane. I dutifully slid the cane free, then tenderly licked his swollen asshole clean. My mouth tingled as much as my hole did where Glen was now washing me the same way.

He pressed his ass back against my face as he once more kissed my throbbing hole. As our pulses slowed, he turned and snuggled into my arms. His hat had fallen off somewhere during the festivities. When he worked the cock ring off, I threw it and those damn jingle bells across the room. We lay there for a long time, watching the fire and kissing, and laughing when we squirmed at the stimulation in our assholes. It felt good holding him, even though I wasn't tired.

Actually, I wasn't tired at all. And when we kissed, I tasted a hint of mulled wine spices from my cock on his lips, along with the peppermint.

"You know," I said, rubbing my fingers in the sticky come and candy juice on his belly. "It's not really that late."

His laugh told me he'd been thinking the same thing. "I'll bank the fire. But no fucking at the party. I have no idea how the peppermint affects rubbers." At my raised eyebrows, he shrugged and grinned. "No matter who you have sex with tonight, I want you feeling my love juice burning your ass. Just like I feel yours." He gave me a quick kiss, then bent to pick up his goblet.

"Merry Christmas, sweetie. Let's go find us a holiday orgy."

Melting
Savannah Stephens Smith

Wintertime. Rain. Endless gray, moss creeping over the driveway, and water dripping like a sad lullaby. Coastal living can be
good. We rarely have to shovel our driveways or creep along
behind a plow truck, shivering and anxious to get home. It's
a gardener's and golfer's paradise, and lovely most of the year.
But winter's rains dampen more than the ground.

By early December, I felt as sodden and dispirited as the
weather. After shaking off my umbrella to the sound of rain
falling endlessly on the carport roof, I closed the door against
another long week. Another lonely Friday night awaited: a
bottle of white wine and the choice between television and
a good novel.

I called my mother on Saturday morning while laundry
tumbled in the dryer. As we talked, I realized I missed winter,
real winter. I missed the cold, blue light against the walls in

the morning when I woke up, a cool brightness that meant there was fresh snow on the ground. I missed the clarity of winter days and the change of seasons. I even missed that hard, flat sky when you could, if you tried really hard, smell the coming snow in the air. My grandfather could always smell snow, and I was convinced that I could, too. I missed the soft hush of snow as it fell silently and turned the ordinary magical. Cold flakes melting on my tongue and the silvery play of moonlight on ice. I even missed ducking snowballs thrown by my brother and sister.

I decided right then.

I was going home for Christmas.

I hadn't seen my folks since summer, and though my brother and sister still lived in our hometown, I knew my parents would like to see us all there. This year, I didn't have a boyfriend to argue with over where we'd spend the holidays or what we'd do, so it was easy to plan my small-town Christmas with the family.

Shopping was almost fun, making a list and checking it not twice but three times, spending a bit too much. But I was single without kids. I packed the trunk of my car with boxes wrapped in red, green, and gold. Then I drove from the wet green to white, from the coast and into the mountains. Just me, the road, and music. There was no one to argue with over the CDs, and no one to complain if I felt like singing along. Loudly. I came out of the low, gray clouds and into the still blue and white of winter. Winter, the way it's supposed to be. Each curve of the highway brought a new postcard-perfect scene, and I was lucky with the weather, passing through only an hour or so of falling snow. The highway was open all the way, vehicles ahead sweeping the roads clear.

I slept that night in my old room, the road curving behind

my closed eyes. Now, it was less my childhood haven and more my mother's crafts-and-computer room. But my old bed was still there, and the same pink and white lamp cast a warm and familiar light.

It was good to be back, to see my family again, to eat at the same old kitchen table, to hear the latest gossip on the neighbors and the people I'd gone to school with.

After dinner on my second day in town, I did the dishes and then went for a walk. The snow was crunchy, like clean, white linen, reflecting light from the moon and the streetlights. It was quiet, and there was hardly any traffic. You don't appreciate a small town until you live in the edgy, anonymous city.

It was more than just an evening walk—I was on my way to the liquor store. The folks usually don't stock anything stronger than orange juice. I'd forgotten to bring anything with me and planned to pick up some rum and rye. I'd discreetly keep it in my room, and it would feel pleasantly naughty to have my evening tipple. There's nothing like thinking that you're breaking a taboo to make things more fun.

I enjoyed the walk, bundled up against the cold. The liquor store was still open, its windows adorned with garlands. I was hesitating over Gibson's Finest versus Seagram's, when I looked up, stopped breathing, and fell back in time.

High school. Ten... no, fifteen years ago.

A long time.

I was a teenager again, trying not to gawk at the object of my girlish desire, yet unable to look away. I was sixteen, the years gone like October's leaves, staring at a boy I had a crush on. A crush? It felt like True Love, and there's no desire more painful or poignant than the unrequited kind. The boy? Oh, he was cute, smart, and athletic, too. He had a mischievous grin and brown hair, and his dad was a lawyer. The boy was popular but still a nice guy. Nice guys seemed rare in the sometimes-vicious world of adolescence. He was dreamy in eleventh grade. I adored him.

I closed my eyes quickly, then opened them again. Yes. Tom Donnelly. Right there in the hometown liquor store. All grown up.

And looking as good as ever.

The years since I trailed him in the high school halls, just happening to be where he was, had been kind to him. Back then, he didn't know I existed. I noticed everything about him (and wrote about it obsessively in my diary), but I was invisible to him. He was a nice guy, and if he didn't take in the quiet girl with the brown hair and glasses, he still smiled when I squeaked "Hi" to him and didn't seem to notice I spent far too much time in the bleachers of the gym, pretending to study but really studying him. In the cafeteria, I'd hear only his voice, and sigh when he would finish lunch with his friends and leave. I was an awkward bundle of mute longing amid the raucous shouts and hoots. All those teenage hormones, cooped up in the same big room during long winter lunch hours.

It seemed like just last week.

I remember how a miasma of grease from the French fries hung in the air, along with whatever was served the day before, adding to the ghost of all lunches past. I remember watching Tom, yearning for him, vividly imagining ridiculous scenarios that would bring him to the realization that I was his True Love. There were other scenarios, too, ones as steamy as my virginal little brain could conjure. I remember how those feelings confused me and put my body in turmoil, and just how fierce that longing was.

Nothing since then has been like that.

We actually became friends his last year of high school. I followed him into auditions for the school musical, trying out just to be near him, and got a small part. I didn't have to sing or dance much, but there were agonizingly sweet hours of rehearsal with the cast. Just friends, for he always had a girlfriend, but it was still infinitely better than staring at him from the bleachers or across the cafeteria.

We lost touch after high school. He graduated, leaving me with a nice enough boyfriend of my own. I went to the coast for university, leaving both my boyfriend and small-town life behind. Tom went north to work. And though our parents stayed in town, we hadn't met up again. Not before that night in the liquor store.

Tom. I stared at him for a minute, clutching my choice (I'd decided on Gibson's) as he waffled between Okanogan whites. Watching him, I felt much the same as I had back then; only this time there was a low wave of wanting, a quickening awareness of the crevice and hollow between my thighs. I'd been cold but not anymore. And now, I knew what those feelings meant, even if the strength of the reaction caught me off guard. Maybe because it had been a while since I'd had a man. A lot of unspent arousal waited inside me.

He wasn't wearing a wedding ring. He did wear jeans, a shirt, and a winter jacket, with gloves poking out of the pockets like they were waving at me. *Hi, Stephanie.* An ordinary man but a good-looking one. Jesus. He still made my heart trip a quick pitter-patter like it did when I was sixteen. And now he made that sweet spot between my legs start to ache. It hummed a little song to my single self: too long, too long, girl, it's been far too long...

That ache felt fine in a funny kind of way. It was good to feel desire again.

Tom looked up and glanced at me. Then he looked again, recognizing me.

Slowly, a grin spread over his face.

A half-hour later, we were still at the Tim Horton's across the street, sitting in the bright and unromantic light, laughing until it hurt. We were both single, though Tom had a daughter from his now-over marriage.

"Thirteen!" I said, marveling. A teenage daughter.

Both of us were successful in our own ways. Both of us had been around a little, learned a lot. And both of us were home for Christmas with family.

And soon we were both tired of Tim Horton's, with its uncomfortable seats and sparse retiree clientele. "Want another coffee?" Tom asked.

"No, thanks," I said. I looked at my bottle in its brown paper bag.

He caught my glance and grinned. We'd clicked, from laughing hellos at the liquor store and, just as easily, Tom read my mind. "How about one to go, then? And we could...put a splash of what's in our bottle in it. It's too cold to walk, I'll drive you home."

I don't know if it was the chill in the air—the sky was clear and black, and stars that I didn't see in the city were flung across the heavens like spilled glitter. Or maybe it was the attraction that had waited, simmering, for more than fifteen years—but Tom didn't take me home. And I didn't ask him to. I'd called my mother from his cell phone, explaining that I'd run into an old friend, and not to worry. She sounded pleased.

Tom and I drove around town looking at the Christmas lights, sipping our drinks, the spiked coffee in my belly warming me deliciously. He drove slowly as we talked, revisiting all those silly things we'd done, learned, and remembered. I liked sitting in Tom's truck with him, with no particular place to go, touring the landscape of our youth, softened by the mantle of snow, and twinkling everywhere with a million lights.

We covered the town, and once again for good measure, then Tom headed up to the local cemetery, careful on the road. Had it been October, it would have been a delightfully spooky location, but in December, even the headstones were blanketed by white and lost their melancholy. Behind us, the streetlights faded, and ahead, the truck's headlights shone on the white snow and black trees. He pulled off the road and put the truck in park. We sat there, the engine rumbling as he turned it on occasionally, keeping us warm. We looked at the lights of town below, watching the place where we'd grown up put itself to bed for the night. We drank our coffee, generously laced with my booze. It was so quiet.

"More?" I asked, the taste of whiskey and coffee on my tongue.

"Yeah," Tom said.

A moment later, I put my cup on the dashboard, carefully. More. I wanted more. I turned to him and kissed him, and after a moment when I thought I'd made a horrible mistake, he kissed me back. Then we kissed, as if it had been scripted by someone who didn't have the patience for three dates and building innuendo. I was only in town for a visit, and so was he. Why wait? We were both free.

We kissed until the windows of his truck steamed up and I couldn't see the moon or the snow. All my unspent longing was afire. I wouldn't tell him that he was making a dream come true for the girl I used to be. We kissed, slowly stoking the building heat between us, and soon my jacket was open and so was his. Then his hand slid over my breast in a caress, my nipple rising hard in return, even under three layers of clothes. Mine stroked his thigh, and his tongue set me ablaze. Tom was a good kisser.

"More?" Tom asked, at one point, our mouths swollen and tender from kissing. "Do you want more?" Always a nice guy, he was a gentleman now.

"Yes," I said. Christmas was going to come early.

"Here?" he asked.

"I don't care..." I was breathless from kissing. "I can't take you back to my parents' place... Besides, it's like being back in high school."

He grinned. "Getting a second chance at it?"

Second chances. Only now I knew what I was doing. We came together, kissing again, knowing it was going to go further, we just had to work out how to do it in Tom's truck. All that unspent desire swept over me anew. I was wet just from kissing him. I wanted him to know it. I needed him to take me.

No more hesitation. My hand slid higher up his jeans to find his hardness, and he fumbled my sweater up. My nipples pressed against my bra, and he tugged the T-shirt I wore underneath out of my pants. His hand was warm, cupping my breast, and his tongue was wicked and knowing. I craved him. The moon slipped in and out of the bare trees like our hands did in each other's loosened clothes.

Tom had a promisingly generous and hard bulge in his jeans. My fingers returned to it, slipping over it again and again. He got my sweater undone—oh, those maddening winter layers—and fumbled with my bra. If only I had known what the day would bring, I would have chosen something sexier. But you never know when luck's going to turn like silver to gold.

The winter night drifted into scattered sensations of rising pleasure. The metal of his zipper, and his hand warm on my back, slipping the catch of my bra open. Clever Tom. Too horny to shiver, I was delighted by each layer he worked through. I arched forward, my breasts filling his hands. He cupped and squeezed, his mouth on mine, my tongue flickering against his, then parting from his mouth reluctantly. A sigh. His thumb slid over my hard nipples. I fought the snap of his jeans, finally getting it open. Tom let me take my time, as if to make sure it was what I really wanted.

It was.

I slid his zipper down over the eager ridge that tantalized me. Then I was undoing him at last, surprised by boxers, not briefs, and after all that work, his cock sprung out, silky and hard.

Oh, he was nice and big. Tom, at last...

I grasped him, squeezed, and caressed the swollen head, hoping I wasn't hurting him. A groan of pleasure told me I wasn't, answered by another surge of heat between my legs. Stroking him, skin hot with arousal, blood rushed, keeping us warm.

"This is what Tom's cock feels like," I thought. "Now I know, sixteen years later."

The moon slipped away. Night was darker and everything was sensation that delighted me, from my bared nipples, my belly, to the hot nugget of want that was my clit. Finding our naked skin under all those winter layers was even more enticing. I kissed him while my greedy fingers couldn't keep away from his cock. "Touch me," I demanded, and Tom obliged with more. He leaned in to suckle at my nipples, and I saw the bare, black trees through the condensation on the windows as his tongue darted circles around my nipples and rasped over the tops. The gravestones slumbered in the snow, and heat licked at my skin. My panties were damp and getting damper. Snow began to fall, flakes drifting to settle against the glass. Melting, just like me.

I wriggled around on the seat of his truck, as horny as I'd been at fifteen, sixteen, seventeen, as Tom's mouth moved back and forth on each breast. He had a trick or two, like taking my nipples gently between his teeth and then sliding his tongue slowly over the tops. It made me shudder with want. But I knew what to do with that need. I was slick and ready for him. Swirling desire intoxicated me, and I felt safe in his truck between the dead and the town.

His chest was hairy and pleasingly muscled. I shivered at last, and he fumbled with the key and turned the engine on again. Snow fell all around us. I was between worlds: the town below, the mountains behind us, and in the middle, Tom's truck. The past and now. I didn't need a future.

But I did need to taste his skin. The smooth swell of his cock brushed against my lips, and then my tongue. I gave him a promise: more. I slid my mouth down his shaft, bracing myself with my hands, bumping the steering wheel with my head. I laughed and heard Tom laugh, too. Then I really sucked him, feeling him grow bigger, harder, hearing his groans of pleasure. His hands were gentle on my head as I showed him what I'd learned in the last fifteen years. I was wetter. Hotter. How could a simple walk to the liquor store turn out like this? I sucked him, awkward and glorious, Tom's fingers in my hair, then gentle against my neck.

I had to have him.

How the hell were we going to manage this? I pulled away from his cock, leaving it glistening from the wet caress of my mouth, thrusting upward, straining with desire. In the dim of winter night, it looked ready to explode.

I undid my own jeans, and my panties came down. They were white and plain. His hand cupped me, one finger slipped in, and he grunted at the slick wetness, the heat of me. I wasn't cold at all. I wriggled my jeans down farther.

How? Tom knew. "Sit on me," he said, his voice rough with need.

We would manage it. We had to. I squirmed out of my pants, kicking them off, crazy for it. "I hope the local cops aren't patrolling up here," I said.

"Be kind of embarrassing," he agreed. "But worth it."

Tom slid over to the middle of the seat. I put my knee over and straddled him, and bumped my head on the roof of the cab. His erect cock thrust up, touching my wet pussy.

Astride him, his thighs warm and muscled, I loved the way he looked with his shirt hanging open. I stroked his chest and played with his nipples like he had done to me. His cock pressed against me, insistent.

I wanted to slow down, to relish every second of it. Yet I couldn't wait. Tom's hands circled my waist, and my breasts were inches away from his mouth. I wanted him to suck them, and I needed to fuck him. I lifted, then found the swollen head of his cock, and caressed it with my wet, open sex. Slick lips kissed his flesh, then his prick parted them. He thrust his hips, pushing into me. I groaned, and sank down slowly, savoring every inch of his cock as it filled me up. I took him all the way in, then settled hard against him. I gasped in pleasure, squarely planted on his erection. I almost came.

I rocked on him, deliberately, clutching his shoulders, and shamelessly offered my ripe nipples to his mouth. Holly berries and cherries. He sucked them as I rode his cock, the center of everything, all I needed for Christmas. Then I was grinding faster against him, with no sweetness now, only the

raw imperative to keep fucking his cock. My throbbing soft-
ness moved against his hardness, seeking the friction I needed.
He was slick from me, but each stroke took me closer and
closer to release.

Then I soared, right there in Tom's truck, in the silent falling snow. My body clenched around his cock like a fist, the
rhythm of coming like bells tolling to drown out the world.
Pleasure so fierce I could turn Christmas into July. I sobbed
something as bliss seized me—I don't know what—and just
let it engulf me.

Tom grabbed me and he bucked beneath my body, seizing
his turn, taking me.

He fucked me from beneath, pumping up deliberately,
then catching the urgency I'd felt. Then he was on the verge. I
felt his intensity deepen, heard his cry, and saw his face change
at the moment of release.

And it was good to feel his pleasure, with my body, with
all the woman I was on that night and the girl I had been. The
one who'd wanted him so badly all those years ago.

We'd fogged up the windows, and it must have been after
midnight. Christmas Eve.

We dressed quickly, complicated tangles of clothes and
laughing acrobatics in the front seat. We drank a final toast
to Christmas wishes and the past years with another shot of
whiskey. The coffee was long gone, but it didn't matter.

It was only a few minutes drive back to my parents' house.
Tom kissed me good night, and as I walked up the driveway,
falling snow still changed the world. The colored lights and
the white lights everywhere cast a glow that matched how I
felt inside.

Tom didn't promise to call me, and I didn't ask him to.

I lingered on the front steps a while, clutching my brown

bag, sitting like I had as a kid, reluctant to go inside. I was cold, but I didn't care. I could hear voices inside the house and my parents' stereo faintly from the living room. It sounded like they had the *Jazz Christmas* album playing. It was nice. I knew I should go inside and be sociable, but I just wanted a few more minutes alone in the quiet, magic night.

That was five months ago. Now, it's spring already, and the big city that I returned to after Christmas is long past the cold and black nights of winter. Trees are budding green, the afternoons are warm, and I noticed my neighbor mowed his lawn last Sunday.

It's been crazy at work, and I've been busy at home, too. That snowy evening in Tom's truck reminded me of what I'd been missing, and I vowed I'd get out more, even if only with girlfriends. You never know.

I started meeting friends for drinks, a movie, a walk in the park, despite the grinding schedule at the office. I've dated a little, but haven't met anyone special.

It took a while, but I finally noticed the box of Kotex under the bathroom sink was sitting there untouched. Sometimes you're so busy doing and thinking of other things, you don't notice that you haven't had a period in two months. Then three. Then I knew.

I hope it's a girl. I've crossed my fingers for a girl, just because I don't know how I'll cope with a boy. Boys are snakes and mud puddles, toy guns and other things I don't understand. But I do understand that things happen, sometimes for a reason and sometimes not.

It's my choice, and I've made it. Part of that choice is that Tom will never know what his best Christmas gift was, on that snowy night.

Stocking Stuffers
T.C. Calligari

Sylvie was curious about Santa. It was the end of the second week, still not quite mid-December, and she was bored. Santa had to be, too; there weren't many kids coming through yet, as parents didn't want to build the fever too soon.

Which meant Sylvie needed to create her own fun. She'd volunteered to do her part for charity, but being Santa's elf was more tedious than she had imagined.

But Santa, well, he was an enigma. Was he old or young, fat, slim or muscular? Sylvie only ever saw him as Santa: big belly, fleecy white hair and beard, and the crimson suit trimmed in white fur. The elves had complementary outfits: The guys were in knee-high black boots, red shorts with suspenders, tight shirts under little red jackets with white fur trim. The girls, Janine and Ashley, besides Sylvie, wore black, high-heel ankle boots, short red skirts trimmed with fur and with suspenders, and the same tight shirts and little jackets with a flounce. The elves were there to help put out the wrapped stocking stuffers for each child after their visit with Santa, and to give parents something to look at while their kids were waiting.

Sylvie walked back behind the curtains to grab a few more gifts. There was curly-headed Ian kneeling in front of Kevin and pulling down his shorts, nuzzling into the hardening bulge.

Sylvie stopped and rolled her eyes. "Must you do that here?"

Ian turned to look at her, Kevin's cock firmly in his hand. "Jealous, honey?"

She sighed, "Yes."

Kevin laughed and guided Ian's head back to idolizing his growing prick.

"Just keep it down," she muttered. "You don't want to scare anyone who might happen up to see Saint Nick."

Kevin smiled, his eyes closing as he leaned back. Ian's mouth made a moue and slowly opened as he slid Kevin's cock toward his throat.

Sylvie just had to watch for a bit. The boys had been picked for their physiques and looks, and she couldn't help but admire Kevin's muscular thighs as he leaned against the wall, his bald head shining like polished marble. Ian's angelic head of curls slid slowly back and forth, his mouth distended about an amazingly thick penis, moaning in pleasure.

They obviously weren't worried about anyone watching, but Sylvie turned away. She was getting too hot. Maybe she could pass that on to Santa, see how bothered he would get. After picking up a few packages wrapped in "boys" gift wrap, she pushed out past the velvet curtain. Santa was just sitting there watching people walk up and down the mall. Nobody was coming up the red carpet at the moment.

Packages for the boys went to Santa's left, and for the girls, to his right. Sylvie crossed in front of him and turned her back, then bent from the waist to put the packages down. She took her time, knowing that in that position the short skirt revealed her white fishnet tights over the white G-string and, consequently, her buttocks. Several times she rearranged the packages to make sure Santa couldn't miss the view, and then stood when she heard a child scampering up the ramp. She spun and flounced past Santa, giving him a wink. He stared at her and had to work hard to tear his gaze away to the little boy who fidgeted in front of him.

He did have the most amazing blue eyes. It made sense, since Saint Nick hailed from an icy realm to the north. Still, what did Santa, or the man beneath, really look like? Was he worth Sylvie working him up? Could she get him to melt? She had asked Ian what Santa looked like, but Ian said they usually left before Santa took off his belly and beard in the change area. Tomorrow, she would have to up the ante, to see if Santa would lose his cool.

The next day, Sylvie wore black fishnet tights for better contrast with her olive skin, and no underwear. It was only a Tuesday and still slow, so how far could she entice Santa? She had to be careful; it might not end up to be the fun game she wanted.

In the afternoon, the photographer arrived. This was after Sylvie had flounced by Santa a few times, bending down in just the right way to give a glimpse or more of her fishnetted thigh or hip. A perfect time for a group photo for publicity. Ashley, Ian, and Janine were away, so it would only be Kevin,

Michael, and Sylvie. The photographer arrived just after the busy lunch hour and started directing them into their places. He wanted a frolic-filled picture, so Kevin was asked to lean over Santa's left shoulder, holding a gift aloft. Michael knelt at Santa's feet, staring out at the crowd, and Sylvie propped herself across Santa's right knee. She perched, really, because she needed to lean out and forward. Santa's arm helped hold her in place, and she realized his hand gripped her thigh.

As the photographer positioned everyone, Sylvie felt Santa's fingers squirm under her thigh. With no underwear, the fishnets were little barrier, and she felt a warm flush start to spread through her limbs. Santa's finger nuzzled through the fishnets, tearing a hole, now delving into the gathering wet of her sex. She didn't dare move for fear of drawing attention, but Santa was a sneaky one. He waited till the photographer was directing someone before he burrowed a bit deeper.

"All right, folks, one last one for fun. You," he pointed at Sylvie, "the female elf. Stay where you are but put an arm around Santa's neck. Place your cheek beside his and give us a big smile."

As Sylvie made the small adjustment and pressed her cheek to Santa's fuzzy beard, his finger made the last maneuver, tearing the fishnets a bit more and slid inside her. Her whimper was barely audible, and she whispered, "Oh, Santa," as the photographer snapped the last shot.

They all stood, except Santa, and Sylvie felt the slow withdrawal of his finger as she stood. She shivered, with the waves of pleasure still moving through her. Santa casually looked over at her and then licked his finger, giving a hearty "Ho-ho-ho" after.

Sylvie went behind the curtain since Michael would spend the next shift out front with Santa. She grabbed Kevin's arm and asked, "Are you sure you've never seen Santa without the outfit?"

A wicked little smile played over Kevin's face. "Well, he's jovial, has white hair..."

She gave him a light smack on his arm. "No, smartass. The guy playing Santa. Any idea what he looks like under the getup?"

Kevin gave her a look. "Sorry, honey, he's always last into the lockers to change, and we're usually gone by the time he removes the mystery. So just what are you checking on your list?"

She shrugged. "Nothing, really. Just curious."

"Naughty or nice?" Kevin laughed and went back to get some gifts.

On Wednesday, Sylvie had the late shift until store closing. Ashley and Ian were also in. When she walked out front, Santa smiled at her and said, "Well, if it isn't my favorite elf. I have something for you." He held up a small, flat, rectangular package.

"What's this?" Sylvie asked.

"Just a little stocking stuffer for being such a good elf. To replace what I damaged."

She raised an eyebrow, then smiled and went behind the curtain to open it. She removed the paper to find a pair of fishnet stockings, black and silky, to replace the tights he'd torn. They came with a lace garter, much sexier than the tights had been, though they had their own mystery. Just imagining wearing the stockings gave Sylvie a little thrill and made her legs tremble with anticipation. Santa couldn't go much further than he did yesterday, and Sylvie was willing to toy with him a bit more.

During her break in the early evening, she changed, getting a little moist at the thought of wearing nothing but the stockings and the short skirt. She had also worn a red satin bustier under her shirt and decided to take the shirt off and stow it in the locker. The top three buttons of the jacket, she left undone, just giving a peek of curving breasts, no more. She couldn't get too risqué.

The rest of the evening passed with enough kids coming through that Sylvie could only give Santa an occasional, tantalizing view. The mall started to clear, and they shut down the North Pole booth, putting away the gifts and other items, closing the curtains and turning off the lights. Everyone else had left, and Sylvie was about to go to the change rooms. She sat for a moment on one of the sorting tables, taking a sip from a glass of water, when Santa entered.

Her heart gave a little thump when he stopped and looked at her and walked over. What would he do?

He began to remove his gloves and said, "Ah, there's my elf. Did you enjoy my stocking stuffer?" He moved closer to her and stood right in front, nearly touching Sylvie.

Not feeling quite so bold suddenly, she stopped swinging her legs and said, "Yes, thank you, very nice."

"And are you wearing it?" Before she could reply he moved forward, pushing her knees apart with his body and placing a hand on either side of her thighs, under the skirt. His thumbs ran over her hipbones, and her breath caught. He ran a hand down the outside of one thigh and then up the inside. His other hand came away for a moment.

As his hand moved to the top of her stocking, tickling the flesh there, Sylvie tried to slow down the action. "Why don't you remove that beard and belly?"

He smiled, his icy blue eyes twinkling. "What makes you

think they're not real?" And his hand slid farther up between her legs.

Sylvie bit her lip as his fingers brushed over her pubic curls. "No one has hair like that," she gasped.

He moved as close as the table would allow, one hand now burrowing into her cleft. "Ah, but you wouldn't want to open your present too soon." He wiggled his hips and pushed her legs farther apart. Sylvie felt she was slipping and set the drink down, reaching out to grab his shoulders, whether to hold him off or pull him close, she wasn't sure. But before she could complete the move, he pulled her to the edge of the table so only her buttocks rested on it. She was only stopped from falling by her legs being around him and his hands on her hips.

Sylvie started to protest when Santa pressed his lips, synthetic beard and all, over hers, and then she felt the heat slide between her labial lips. The hard bulb of his cock slid over her clit, and down, slicking her with desire.

She wrestled with herself. Who was he under the beard and red suit? He could be anyone: the geeky courier guy at the lab where she worked, her mailman, the angry neighbor who lived below her. Sylvie's rational thoughts were losing to the slippery pleasure pushing against her pussy. Wasn't it just a bit more naughty, not knowing the true face of the man about to fuck you? And she had started the whole escapade.

He pushed at the same time as he pulled her forward, a hand around each thigh. Sylvie gasped, then moaned, losing her weak fight with temptation. Her stocking-clad legs went around Santa's suit, belly padding and all. Then he lifted her off the table and slowly embedded his thick, hot cock in her slick cunt. She slid down, her vaginal muscles clamping in spasms of ecstasy, and it was his turn to moan.

Impaled on his cock, Sylvie clung to his neck for a moment, her face buried in the fake white hair. Beneath it, she could smell a muskiness reminiscent of earth and trees. A wild, healthy scent. She groaned into the beard, hoisting herself up on his delicious rod, to slide down again.

It wasn't an easy position, but he held her and helped lift her to slide down again. Sylvie trembled as much from the exertion as from the heat emanating from her core. One last ember of reason had her pant out, "Won't we get locked in?" before they succumbed to a piston play of lust and muscle.

Up he hoisted her, and down she slid, again and again, the heat of their friction slicking them both with her juices. Sylvie tore at his hair, dislodging hat and wig and beard—but not seeing, for the haze of passion and heat blurred her vision in the low light.

They moved in rhythm, up and down, in and out, their breaths gasping as one, their sweat mingling, moans joining as their flesh fit each other perfectly. Sylvie's eyelids fluttered as her heart hammered loudly. Her whole body shivered and clasped his as her orgasm erupted. He convulsed and thrust harder into her, and light exploded behind her eyes…a thousand shattering snowflakes, sparkling points of pleasure and passion cascading around them, slowly settling, as the vibrations of their bodies slowed.

As her senses returned, Sylvie realized it was the moment of truth. Her face was still buried near his neck, but she had torn away the disguise. Slowly, she pulled back and sighed, then opened her eyes. Santa stood before her or now, rather, a man in a Santa suit. He had black hair and those amazing blue eyes. His chin was slightly pointed, and his eyebrows had a nearly elfin upswing at the corners. He smiled at her.

"Well, my little elf, you unwrapped your present a little early."

"Mmm." She closed her eyes for a moment as he sat her back on the table top and pulled out of her. "I thought that it was you who unwrapped your present first. But we should get going. We'll be locked in for sure now."

He zipped up and then removed the Santa belly, revealing a trim, not overly muscular body. Sylvie liked the look of her present, and a flush of relief ran through her. "Oh, we don't have to be worried about that. I'm head of security for the mall. I just volunteered to help out."

She laughed and said, "Me, too. The volunteering, that is. I work at the lab across the street. This elf's name is Sylvie."

He dropped the padded belly and came up to her and kissed her, "Well, elf Sylvie, I'm Michel, and thank you for such a lovely stocking stuffer. If you play your cards right, there could be a few more early presents before the big day." He helped her off of the table, his warm hands nearly encircling her waist.

Sylvie laughed again and straightened her clothes. "Oh, really? Don't you have a list, and aren't you checking it twice?"

Michel cocked his head to the side. "Most definitely, and you're in both columns. Naughty and nice. So what say we get changed and I'll buy you a few drinks?"

Sylvie nearly wriggled with delight. It was going to be a very good Christmas, indeed.

Dangerous Fruitcake
Anonymous

"Don't be mean," you tell me. "You know she loves us."

"Of course, she does," I say, tearing open the package. "That's why she sends us the same thing every Christmas."

The package comes open, and I sit there regarding another fruitcake, a rock-solid block of snail-mail granite.

"She bakes it herself!" you say defensively. You're so protective of your aged grandmother—even her fruitcakes.

"Of course, she does," I say.

"You've got to taste it fresh," you mutter sadly. "It's delicious."

"I'm sure it's nice when it's fresh."

"It's succulent. Moist and delicious."

I take the fruitcake out of the wrapping, hold it in my hand, pound it against the table.

"Amazing what three weeks in the cargo compartment of a 747 can do to 'moist and delicious.' "

The problem with grandma is that she was raised in the Depression. She mails everything fourth class.

"We have to keep it until Mom comes," you say. "We'll wrap it in cellophane and put it under the tree. It makes her happy to know we got one, too."

"She likes to share the pain."

"Stop," you say. "She means well."

Hefting the deadly fruitcake, I look at you and smile. It's two Saturdays before Christmas, and you're wearing your weekend lounging-in-bed, drinking-coffee-and-reading-*The-New-Yorker* clothes. Long, white T-shirt, thin with wear, damp with sweat from the hot blow of the space heater. Panties underneath, peeking at me invitingly.

"You wouldn't," you say, clutching your *New Yorker* to your chest.

"I would," I say and reach for you.

"Let go!" you shout as I seize your shirt, dragging you into the middle of the bed. You start to giggle as I get my arm under yours and perform a neat wrestling move that you'd never let me get away with if you weren't distracted by the fruitcake. I thrust you over my lap and hold you there, pulling up your long white T-shirt and raising the fruitcake like a paddle.

"Moist and delicious, huh? I'll show you moist and delicious!"

The fruitcake comes pounding down, and you yelp as it strikes your buttocks. Rather than the satisfying *slap!* I'm used to, it makes a dull thudding sound. It makes you giggle.

"You're being difficult," you say sharply, fighting through the giggles. "Stop spanking me with my grandmother's fruitcake!"

"You're the difficult one," I say. "Put your ass in the air and take your spanking like a good girl!"

That brings another giggle, and you snuggle deeper into my lap and lift your ass. I bring the fruitcake down, harder this time, and the thud comes firmly enough to make you gasp. Your ass wriggles as you push it higher. You always did prefer thud to sting, and this is the thuddiest implement of all, its hard-baked exterior hitting hard while its thick, gooey insides provide the weight.

I spank you several more times with the fruitcake, and you're not struggling any more. Now my hand is tangled in your hair, holding your face down against the pillow as I hit your ass repeatedly. I can feel my cock growing, pressing against your breasts. You can feel it, too, and you squirm a little, rubbing it. I spank you three more times in rapid succession, bringing soft moans from your lips. *The New Yorker* falls neglected to the carpet in a flurry of glossy paper. Five more spanks, fast and hard, you whimpering and pushing your ass up to greet my blows. The fruitcake leaves oily stains on your white cotton panties.

"Take them off," I tell you.

This time you don't argue, don't struggle, don't even whimper. You squirm in my lap as you pull down your panties to your ankles and kick them across the room.

"The shirt, too," I tell you firmly.

You pull your arms into the stretched-out armholes and wriggle the shirt up to your head, casting it across the pillow. Now you're naked, your bare bottom red and gorgeous in the slanted morning sunlight.

You gasp as I bring the fruitcake down on your naked behind. You push your ass up into the air again, begging for more. You start whimpering as I strike you faster, my cock surging against your breasts. I feel your hand around it, tucked under your body as you slowly stroke me. You moan, your hand tightening on my cock. Your legs slip open wider, your pussy exposed. I turn the fruitcake sideways and strike your pussy with the narrow edge, bringing a shriek and then a long, low moan of pleasure. I hit it more lightly, the edge striking your clit. It's begun to soften with the repeated abuse, and it's just the right texture for your pussy.

You're gasping now, rubbing my cock as you wag your ass back and forth. I hit your pussy rhythmically, knowing just the right timing to bring you close—but not bring you off. You adjust yourself, bending your waist sharply so you can leave your ass high in the air, and move your face to my cock. You take it into your mouth, bent at an improbable angle as you start sucking my cock. Each stroke of your tongue brings a harder spank, and I alternate between your pussy and your ass. Both are now shiny with sticky sugar, moist and delicious.

The fruitcake breaks open, falling into a half-dozen pieces on the bed. You barely notice, consumed by your desire for my cock. I push you off me and onto your belly, and your ass rises high into the air as I take my place between your thighs.

I scoop up a pulpy mass of the fruitcake's moist insides and reach around to your face, pushing it into your mouth. You accept it hungrily, chewing and savoring the spicy taste as my cockhead finds your entrance and I push swiftly in, feeling you wet. You're so wet, in fact, that I can feel a dribble leaking onto my balls as I slide all the way into you, and I know you're very close to coming.

Another mass of pulpy flesh finds its way into your mouth, and you lick my fingers as I reach under you with my other hand. To make you come hard in this position, my cock has to work slowly, deliberately, each thrust firm and deep, pressing down and into your G-spot. And my fingers, still sticky and oozing with fruitcake mess, have to press hard on your clit. Your ass works back and forth, pushing you onto me rhythmically, telling me I've found exactly the right spot, exactly the right cadence. You're close. I grab a wad of fruitcake and use the mush to cushion my fingers so I can press harder on your clit, the way I might use a pillow.

You lick the pulp from my fingers, biting down almost hard enough to hurt me as you start to come.

The second I feel your pussy spasming, the instant I know you're over the edge, I start fucking you rapidly, the way you love. You're still coming when I reach my own completion, my muscles tensing as I spurt inside you, mingling my come with your grandmother's fruitcake. Your pumping ass goes slack, easing down until you're lying flat on the bed, fruitcake crushed beneath your hips, with me on top of you in an irregular bed of spicy breadstuff with crispy, dried-out edges.

"No fruitcake under the tree this year," I say sadly.

You turn your head so I can kiss you, and I taste the spice of Grandma's fruitcake.

"Mmm," I say. "Moist and delicious."

"I got your moist and delicious right here," you say and reach for me.

Tagged
Sharon Wachsler

I have two rules about tag sales: Always test it out first, and never pay more than ten dollars—for anything. Even if it's a fabulous antique dresser with original patina and mirror. Even if it's a vintage black cocktail dress with hand-beaded hem and feather boa neckline. Even if it's—and yes, God once graced me with this find—an entire Cuisinart set, including not only the food processor with every blade, but bread maker, mixer, and juicer. I got them all, because bottom line—only desperate people hold tag sales. They're stressed about having too much crap, about moving or leaving a relationship or facing bankruptcy, so any bucks are good bucks, and anything they don't have to move lightens their load. Not that they give in happily.

For instance, the bitter divorcé who hawked the Cuisinart extravaganza scowled at my ten-dollar bid before agreeing with a surly, "Yeah, whatever, just get the bitch's crap outta here."

When I told him I'd need an electric outlet to make sure each appliance worked, I thought he might take a swing at me. Through teeth clenched like fists he said, "Extension cord. In driveway," and turned away. Each gadget whirred and whizzed to my satisfaction, and I've been making sage bread and banana daiquiris and hot, fresh salsa ever since. All of which Dana is happy to gobble down and none of which has changed her attitude about what I do on Saturday mornings.

I grew up among a dedicated pack of weekend-morning yard-sale prowlers. That's what we called them—yard sales or tag sales. My lover, Dana, calls them garage sales, when she's in an unusually good mood. Most of the time she calls them "garbage sales."

Needless to say, Dana stays home during my excursions and usually grumbles at every new find I bring back to our nest. I end up feeling like a cat proudly presenting its owner with a dead mouse: no matter how often it happens, I always hope for praise and almost always hear groans, instead. It is rare indeed when I receive a "Now that might actually be useful" (cordless drill and complete set of bits, four dollars). Useful, my ass. Power tools turn Dana on—that's the only reason I buy them. Sure as hell I never use them, and I've yet to see Dana do more than take them out, shine them, and search longingly for something to drill, saw, or sandblast. But the day I surprised Dana with the drill set, she threw me down on the kitchen floor and made love to me like she meant it.

However, there were no mechanics' wet-dream machines on display this cool autumn morning. I wondered at my decision to come out today as I scoured racks of toys and outgrown children's clothes and piles of trashy novels, mismatched dishes, and mugs that said things like WORLD'S

GREATEST DAD. Dana was probably home whacking off and watching a football game, snuggled deep in the comforter on the couch. And here I was, like an idiot, searching for a present for my lover for a holiday I don't even celebrate.

You see, I'm Jewish, so Christmas doesn't mean much to me. But Dana gets melancholy if she doesn't at least have a tree and a couple of gifts on Christmas morning. Our compromise is that we call the tree a "Hanukkah bush" and that I don't have to deal with the crazy lights-and-Santas-everywhere and "Jingle Bells"-blasting-from-every-speaker atmosphere of the mall. I get to find her presents doing what I like best—bargain-hunting on some stranger's lawn.

Now, three months before Christmas, I was scanning the detritus, thinking, "WWSB"—"What would Santa buy?" However, neither the skies nor the wares looked promising as I pulled my windbreaker tighter around my sweater and blew on my hands to warm them. A gang of unruly children raced among the tables and boxes, shooting water from plastic guns at each other and calling, "You're dead!"

"No, you are! I got you first!"

I tried to block out the noise. But it wasn't just the kids causing the ruckus. The sale was packed—SUVs, old Volvos, and pickup trucks were parked end to end on both sides of the street. It was a mob scene—the kind of sale where people clutched their finds to their chests lest they put something down and have it snatched up by another greedy lawn prowler. The harried woman in a blue house dress and pink change apron in the middle of the chaos looked as if she were about to fly apart from trying to keep track of her kids, the strangers in her yard, her money, and all the stuff that must go-go-go.

I was turning to leave, rubbing my arms to increase the circulation, when I saw a black cord trailing from a shoe box

e. Thinking it might be something the Christ-
ch sister had left behind, possibly earning me
nd-eggnog-induced very merry fuck, I went
illed from the box a gray plastic thingy that
led a smooth, mini-version of an elephant's
tion cups on the side and an on/off switch at
ibout to ask pink-apron-lady when I realized
ome-Jacuzzi adapter. You set the thing on the
o and it makes bubbles. It even had an adjust-
heater so you could switch off the bathroom
I warm and frothy in a dim, steamy glow. I'd
:alog once. I'd pointed it out to Dana, raising
:h a suggestive wink-wink, nudge-nudge ex-
'd grunted, "I bet it doesn't even work," and
way.

ey-back guarantee," I pointed out.

e we both supposed to fit in the tub at once?
:hed up. How much fun would that be?"

of us could Jacuzzi while the other gives
d then we could switch. It could be very

er eyes. "Or it could be a waste of money
ie. Besides, what do we need romance for?
er eight years."

That's exactly why we need romance, I'd thought as I'd
returned to my catalog. A quickie on the couch every month
or so during half-time was not exactly fulfilling my womanly
needs, and I was going to get carpal tunnel syndrome from
the vibrator if things kept going the way they were.

Now, standing in the driveway with brown leaves around
my feet, I looked at the strange device. I don't care what Dana
thinks, I grumbled to myself, this could be fun. It might even

be good for her arthritic knee. She wouldn't be bitching then. I was so sick of hearing about her goddamn knee. If she'd just go to a physical therapist or a chiropractor or something, maybe she'd get some relief. Instead she chose complaint therapy, with me as her unpaid therapist. This Jacuzzi thing would make an excellent gift if it helped her knee. I could even pair it with one of those miniature TVs so she could watch the game and soak her pain away at the same time.

There weren't any instructions and I didn't see its original box, so I tucked it under my arm and approached the frazzled homeowner.

"This turns your bath into a hot tub, right?" I asked.

"Yeah," she nodded, "And I've only ever used it once. Christmas present. Nice thought, but who has the time?" She wheeled to bellow at a blond kid. "Christopher, put that down! That is not a toy!"

"Sorry," she said, turning back to me. "Anyway, like I said, it's like new. Do you want it?"

I looked at the red dot on the black power cord. "$18" was scrawled in magic marker. I took in her unkempt hair straggling from its scrunchy, her eyes that constantly skipped to check this child or that, her rumpled change purse. I was sure I could talk her down to ten, maybe even five.

"Well…" I drew out the word, "I'd need to test it out first, make sure it works."

She sighed, "Of course," then shouted to a girl of twelve or thirteen. "Liz! Liz, for goodness sake, pay attention! Get over here." Then, when the girl was at her side, she pointed at me. "Take this lady to the bathroom. She wants to test this out." The woman added in a low voice with stern eyes, "And stay with her. Make sure she doesn't get lost."

We all knew what that meant—make sure she's just testing out the Jacuzzi device, not lifting the silver or casing the joint. The stringy girl shrugged her shoulders and muttered a sulky, "C'mon."

We walked in through the garage, and the teen pointed at a door down a hallway. "There," she said and wandered off.

Well, so much for keeping me from stealing the entertainment system. The girl stomped into what I presumed was her bedroom and slammed the door. The next minute, I heard a loud screeching that I assumed was what was passing for music with today's youth.

I went into the bathroom—which was decorated in blue pastels and strewn with a lot of child-related stuff—and shut the door. Good God, I couldn't believe how cold it was outside, even for October. My fingers were white and frozen. It felt good to be inside, if only for a moment.

I was about to turn on the sink taps to test out the device and heat up my hands when I glanced at the tub to my right. I turned nervously to the door and was reassured by feeling hip-hop or death metal or whatever it was vibrating the little house. What could be the harm? After all, if I really wanted to know if it worked I should test it for real—and warm up at the same time.

I locked the door and turned on the tub's hot-water faucet full blast. I added a bit of cold so I wouldn't sear my skin off, plugged in the Jacuzzinator, and hung it on the porcelain side. Then I quickly whipped off my sneakers, socks, windbreaker, sweater, jeans, bra, and panties. Just the act of stripping naked in a stranger's house was giving me an unexpected thrill. Usually I was such a "good girl." I looked at myself in the full-length mirror on the door, my breasts hanging heavy, and ran my hands up my sides, caressing myself until my nipples got hard and rosy. I rubbed them in circles, then lifted one to my mouth so I could see myself sucking on my tit in the mirror. It was a party trick I'd learned in college, and I liked the way I looked doing it.

Nobody knows I'm in here doing this, I thought, and felt a zing shoot down to my cunt.

I'd shaved my legs just that morning, so I posed à la Betty Grable, leaning over to run my hands up my smooth legs, further turning myself on. I really did look good. Damn, why didn't Dana see it? I let my hands stray further, tickling my pubic hair, delighting in how quickly I became moist. I gave the mirror a sultry stare as I let an index finger slide into my slit. I shivered.

Okay, don't be ridiculous, I told myself. You're not a twenty-year-old stripper, you're a forty-one-year-old social worker with a pot belly. Get to business. Test the damn thing, see if it would make a good Christmas present for Dana, go home.

Despite my little lecture to myself, I was still turned on. I could smell my wetness rising up from between my legs. Maybe my own amorousness would be enough to actually get my lover to tear her eyes from the screen and do me right. At least I'd be all clean and shiny, I thought, turning to the bath.

How had the tub filled so fast? I turned off the taps and slid in.

Ah, I exhaled, it felt great to be warm. I examined the gray plastic device and tentatively pressed a button. Immediately hot water shot out of two tubes near the bottom. One was squirting directly into my face. Sputtering, I groped around, found the tube, and twisted it down. Now it was shooting warm, bubbling water against my submerged thigh. That was nice. I fiddled around and discovered that the tubes could be rotated side to side, as well as up and down.

I was still horny from my earlier self-lovin' striptease. The further trespass of stealing into a foreign tub and soaking—in my own juices, as it were—was just increasing my high. I hung my leg over the side of the tub. Experimentally, I rotated one tube until it was spraying at my submerged clit. Then I set the other one to shoot a hot stream into my cunt.

The bubbles acted like a warm vibrator against my clit. No, I decided, it was better—I didn't have to hold anything, and even if I hadn't been prelubed already, the water would've taken care of that. The heat, the bubbles, the simultaneous feeling of pressure on my clit and driving fullness in my cunt was exquisite. I sank further into the tub and wiggled myself closer to the jets. I could feel my clit swelling, my hole opening, the liquid sensation of sexual delirium flowing down my legs, making my toes tingle. I leaned back, rolling my nipples between my thumbs and forefingers, whimpering blissfully.

The dual streams—their steady momentum against my engorged pussy so much more consistent and luxurious than any lover's manual ministrations could be and more powerful than any tongue—urged me irresistibly forward. I met the water's thrust with my own, lifting and bucking my hips toward the Jacuzzi's mouths. I felt my orgasm rolling in. Knowing that I couldn't scream the way I wanted to made it all the more delicious. With a great gasp that I tried to smother, I came in wave after wave, one hand gripping the tub's side, the other grabbing the soap dish handle.

I leaned back with a groan and turned the jets so they massaged my tummy and bottom. I knew it was ridiculous, but I felt warm and cared for by this inanimate thing. I was luxuriating in the afterglow until I suddenly realized how bad it would look if Liz ever came to check up on me.

I let the water out, tingling all over as I hurriedly toweled off with a clean, blue, terry-cloth bath sheet I'd found in a cubby of linens next to the shower. I threw it into the laundry hamper, donned my clothes, and lifted the appliance from the tub edge.

I sauntered back outside, trying to look nonchalant. There were fewer people at the sale, and I wondered how long I'd been. The sun was starting to sink.

The woman was making change for a man holding a lamp.

"I've decided to take it," I announced to her back. She turned, smiling, then furrowed her brows. I followed her expression. She was studying my hair, I touched it unthinkingly; it was wet up to my ears. Under her scrutiny, my already telltale pink cheeks and nose were turning red. Then she glanced at the house. I looked, too. The bathroom window was completely fogged up. I hadn't thought to towel it dry.

"Right," she said. "That'll be fifty dollars, please."

"Sure thing," I nodded, reaching into my purse.

I headed for my car. I had just the gift for Dana's arthritic knee: a gift certificate for a few sessions with a competent physical therapist. I'd start asking around on Monday.

As for romance, it was overrated. I decided that it was important for me to stop seeking fulfillment from others. My gift to myself was going to be to love myself more—and very often. Oh yes, it was going to be a very Merry Hanukkah for me.

Caught Watching
Saskia Walker

I nearly didn't go to the party. The seasonal celebrations had been rocking on for two weeks already, with office parties, and family and friends to see. I was ready to sidestep this one. Then I reminded myself that my New Year's resolution was to see and do even more. Besides, Natalie insisted I had to go and meet her latest playmate.

Natalie and I worked for the same London media corporation, and her roller-coaster romantic life never failed to capture the attention of her friends. She loved that attention. I didn't quiz her about the new playmate over the phone. Part of the fun was finding out whether the playmate was a playgirl or a playboy.

"Okay, I'll be there." I glanced at my wardrobe dubiously. The party season had severely depleted it, but I managed to find my leather miniskirt and a crop top in the pile of abandoned gear.

The event was being held at a music studio in Camden, and the party was in full swing by the time I got there, the lobby a crush of guests high on seasonal goodwill. A Christmas tree blinked lights in one corner; the framed photographs and discs on the walls were adorned with decorations. Natalie rushed through the crowd when she spotted me, all tumbling dark hair and luscious curves in a PVC bodice and skirt. Around her neck she wore a froth of silver tinsel, boa-like. She hugged me and led me into the main room, where people were dancing. She grabbed me a glass of wine and then took me over to a lean punk with a crown of bleached hair.

"This is Idol," she announced. "Well, that's the name she goes by and I think it suits her, don't you?"

It did suit her. The woman's combination of power and wariness made her both distant and desirable. I nodded and smiled, eyeing her body, perfectly outlined in a simple white T-shirt and jeans. Heavy work boots completed her look.

"Don't ask her real name," Natalie added. "She won't tell anyone, not even me."

Idol draped herself against Natalie, possessively. She gave me a wicked smile and then drew Natalie away onto the crowded dance floor. Natalie wrapped her tinsel boa around Idol's neck, shimmying it as they danced. That was cute. And sexy. Natalie waved and winked at me. She was simmering, visibly. I watched Idol's hand moving around Natalie's hips and smiled back, inspired by their flagrant sexuality.

I drank my wine and edged round the party, chatting with people I knew from the office. When I remembered to check my lipstick, I couldn't find any obvious signs to the bathroom. Gloomy corridors and storerooms branched off from the studios in all directions. I investigated cautiously, the noise of the party receding as a door closed behind me. At the end of the corridor an oblong of light drew my attention. As I got closer, I heard laughter.

"No, I want to wear it." It sounded like Natalie.

I paused when I could see into the room. It wasn't the ladies' at all, it was an office, and the two inhabitants obviously weren't expecting company. Idol was sitting on a high-backed chair, entirely naked. Natalie was standing in front of her, holding a strap-on cock in one hand.

I stepped back, hiding in the darkness.

Idol smiled up at Natalie and put down her wine glass. Lifting her legs she hung them over the arms of the chair. In that one swift move, she exposed the thatch of fair hair over her pubic bone and the glistening slit beneath. She ran one finger over her clit.

I glanced back down the passageway. Could I risk going back, or would they hear me? I realized I had inadvertently become a spectator to a private show. And now Natalie had unzipped her skirt and was stepping out of it.

She was wearing high-heeled boots, stockings and garters, no panties. The pale globes of her ass contrasted starkly with the black garters and stockings. The abandoned tinsel boa trailed on the floor. Somewhere nearby people were singing Christmas songs in drunken, laughter-filled voices. It was like a debauched Christmas-card vision of sex and celebration. I couldn't look away; the scene transfixed me.

Natalie bent over, the strap-on hanging loosely in one hand, like a loaded gun. She tongued Idol's clit, and Idol was wired. "Put it on," she demanded, impatiently.

Natalie climbed into the strap-on, pulling the holster tight against her pussy and between her ass cheeks. She knelt down, one hand on the rigid cock, the other cupping one of Idol's pert breasts. She captured the swollen nipple between her thumb and forefinger, her mouth on the other nipple, sucking heavily.

Idol's head began to roll from side to side against the back of the chair. "Hurry," she pleaded. Natalie began to ease the head of the cock into her slippery hole, spreading Idol's juices over it as she went. "Oh, God," Idol moaned. "It's huge."

Natalie chuckled. "I know, but you're going to have to take it, honey." She worked her hips slowly, edging it deeper inside, her hands going to the arms of the chair to brace herself.

Idol began to rock, her eyes wide. "Fuck, it's right there," she whimpered, her hips moving.

My breathing tripped. I'd heard a sound behind me. Before I had time to turn around, an arm grabbed me around the waist and a hand fell over my mouth. My heart missed a beat. I was hauled back against a body that enveloped mine.

"Well, well, what have we here, a naughty little voyeur?" The question was breathed low against my ear, followed by a dark chuckle. I reacted, my fingers pulling at the hand over my mouth. The man seized me tighter still, drawing me back and deeper into the shadows, a warning note in his voice. "Stay quiet. You wouldn't want to interrupt them, would you, not when she is so close to coming?"

Even if I could speak, what could I say?

I shook my head. After a moment, the hand slipped away from my mouth. I breathed deeply, glancing back. In the gloom, I saw a flash of high cheekbones and hooded eyes, watchful and sparkling with humor. My face flamed at the idea of being caught watching by this man, this stranger. A rather attractive stranger, I noticed. He put one finger to his lips and then pointed me back toward the scene. I obeyed, my attention torn between the women and the dominating presence of the man standing so close behind me.

"Stay quiet..."

I started, but smiled, when his hands found their way around me. The scent of his musk, like warm nectar, seduced me. While he watched over my shoulder, he ran his fingers against my throat, the other hand drawing my body tight against his. He caressed the outline of my breasts through my top. I fought the urge to moan aloud. His fingers tightening on my nipples wired them into the heat between my thighs, creating a molten loop of tension through my body.

In front of us, Idol began to groan, loudly. Her hips plunged on the glistening cock.

I was on fire with arousal. I thrust my hips back against him. He was rock hard. His hands moved to my skirt, shifting the leather on my hips. A pang of deviance deep in my core roared its approval. Yes, I wanted him to lift my skirt, to touch me. I reached down and shimmied the leather up.

He reacted—turned me in his arms, backing me to the wall, his fingers pressing my G-string into my damp slit. He bent to kiss me, his mouth opening me up, making me melt. I lifted one leg along his flank, letting him in. His hips ground against my pussy, lifting me bodily. Hot need welled inside me, my clit sparking.

"You're on fire," he whispered against my lips.

"Do it. Quickly," I urged.

I heard his fly, the rasp of a condom wrapper. Pushing my G-string aside, he lifted me, his hands warm and sure on my buttocks. Easing me down, I was filled—inch-by-inch—with hot, hard cock.

He began to grind—shallow moves, deep inside. I was powerless to do anything but clutch at his shoulders and ride it out, sensation exploding through me each time he hit home. I reached down to feel his girth where we were joined, and he groaned. I rubbed my clit with the heel of my hand, my fingers crooked around the base of his cock. He inhaled sharply, his cock pounding inside me. I was about to explode. Over his shoulder I saw Idol grasp feebly at Natalie's arms, where they were braced on the chair. Her hips bucked wildly, out of control.

I was right there and he knew it. He rammed up inside me. I closed my eyes, crushed my clit and bit my lip, hot spasms rolling out from my core. His cock jerked inside me, making me shudder, boneless with pleasure.

As the heat ebbed away, I realized Idol was getting dressed. We had split seconds before we were discovered.

He noticed, too. "I want to see that deviant look in your eyes under brighter lights," he whispered, and nodded toward the party. He lowered me to the floor, raising an eyebrow suggestively.

I nodded, smiling. Well, my New Year's resolution had been to see and do even more, hadn't it?

Hollywood Christmas
Thomas S. Roche

It's not exactly our first date; we already went out for coffee once. But that was during the day, and this is at night—a hot night right before Christmas, pulsing with all the energy of West Hollywood when it's 80 degrees here and snowing in the rest of the world. There's a Christmas party up on Mulholland, at the big house of a friend you met when you were dancing, some closeted movie-industry semi–big shot. Jacob is his name, but you won't tell me his last name because you're quite sure I'd recognize it. "He's very secretive," you tell me conspiratorially. "You have to be, when you work in Hollywood."

I dread the thought of going to the movies right before Christmas, and a dinner out wouldn't quite be celebratory enough for us, so I'm relieved you suggest the party.

From the moment we park the car I can see the house is packed with young queer guys. As I get out of the car, three of them come up to you, their eyes lazing over me. They shriek your name, hug you, kiss you, let their eyes linger on me.

You introduce one as Aaron, tell Aaron my name as the other guys kiss you and drift away.

"Who's the hunk?" Aaron asks. "Does he play for our team? We can always use another pitcher with perfect biceps." He reaches out and squeezes mine.

"He's mine," you say with mock testiness, and you and Aaron kiss again, this time on the lips. He says something in French to me and drifts off with his friends.

"You don't mind, do you?" you say as we mount the stairs toward the throbbing music.

"Looked like a platonic kiss to me," I say.

"No, no," you tell me. "I mean you don't have a problem with guys flirting with you, do you?"

I shrug. "Did David have a problem with Michelangelo?"

You giggle. "Not a great metaphor, isn't that what your last review said?"

I jab you in the stomach and you giggle more. I go on tickling you all the way up the stairs, a convenient excuse for us to press our bodies together. I wonder if it seems like I'm trying to look straight. I don't care, because the feeling of your body against mine is making my dick hard in my jeans, and I'm more afraid you'll notice that than that my attempts to surreptitiously grope you will seem like conspicuous heterosexuality. By the time we make it in the door, my hand is around your waist and my fingertips tucked just under your waistband on that magnificent curve of your hip. You've got one finger hooked in my belt loop.

We walk past some guys barbecuing on the front porch. Big, thick sausages sizzle on the grill, phallic delights that look pasty-gray and smell vegan. One of the guys, a bald, goateed guy, looks at me, then the sausages, then me again. He winks.

"Hungry?" he asks.

"Not yet," I deadpan. "Maybe later."

You introduce me around, subjecting me to a whirlwind of faces and names I don't take note of and won't remember. There are a few women, two of them in the dozen people you introduce me to. At least one of them clearly didn't start her life that way, and the other makes it quite clear that she's at least as interested in you as I am. You can't find your friend to say hello, so "I'm parched," you say, and drag me toward the punch bowl.

The punch bowls are marked: "Magic" and "Not Magic." You pour us each a cup of the mundane kind. From the saucered eyes shimmering wildly in the sweating press of male bodies in the enormous living room, which has been cleared of furniture to better facilitate the surge and seethe of flesh to the loud house music, the other kind is dangerously magical.

"Ugh," you say as you take a drink. "I hate vodka." Then you finish the punch in one gulp like you were slamming down shots. Over the punch bowl, you press your lips to mine like my tongue's a lime to complement your tequila. I taste $30-a-bottle vodka and $1-a-gallon fruit punch. Your tongue has a post through it. You're a damn good kisser.

You pour yourself another cup of punch, and I daintily sip mine as I realize with puzzlement that the pulsating music is a techno version of "The Little Drummer Boy." It bleeds into a grinding happy-hardcore "Carol of the Bells" with the sounds of men orgasming mingled conspicuously with about 180 beats per minute.

"Fuck the fruit punch. Let's dance," you say.

I shoot my punch and wince, then follow you obediently

out to the dance floor, your finger still hooked in my belt loop, this time one right in front, dangerously close to my zipper. I feel my cock swell at your touch. We have to practically wedge ourselves in among the dancers, bodies pressing us so tight that we're almost in full contact as we grind and squirm. I reach back and move my wallet to my front pocket. You put your arms around my neck and pull my face close to yours. I kiss you and let my hands curve around your waist. You're wearing one of those trendy, slutty shirts that shows off your belly, and as I let my hands creep back I feel the top of your thong showing over your low-slung jeans, which I noticed a long time ago. It makes me want to slide your pants off of you. Instead, I just tuck my fingers into your waistband, letting them squeeze between the very top of your buttocks and the stretched fabric of your jeans. If I still had any doubt about whether you were going to fuck me, which I didn't, it would be dispelled by the way you react to my touch on your ass. Pushing back, squirming against my hands, the jaunty angle of your body bringing your tits into contact with my upper body while you kiss me deeply, your pierced tongue working into my mouth as your nipples harden against my chest and your ass grinds into my hands. I'm so hard I know you can feel it, smell it, taste it, even though your body isn't pressing against me that low. But a moment later, your hands are, your fingers working the bulge in my pants as you pull back and look into my eyes.

I lean over, speaking into your ear. "You call this dancing?" I ask.

Your lips brush my ear, and you say it low, husky, a hungry invitation.

"No. I call this foreplay."

Then you kiss me on the lips again and massage my cock,

grinding your ass back into my hands. Your pants are so tight that as I wedge my hands in, I feel one button of your fly go popping open. That only makes you kiss me harder, stroke my cock harder. I don't even bother looking around to see if guys are watching us. I can feel their bodies pressed against us, smell their arousal. I can feel the whole dancing mass grinding together in a way that spells sex, and I'm sure more hands than just ours are wandering. If the guys aren't watching, it's because most of them are too blasted or too busy. But the tightly pressed bodies do provide a perfect cover.

Everything goes black in an instant.

A disappointed sound goes up from the crowd, mingled with shrieks and laughing. It's just a blown circuit breaker, but you take your cue and in a single fluid motion, you've slid your glorious ass out of my grasp. You're down on your knees in front of me.

I've never had a woman get my pants open so fast, but then, you hang out with fags, so perhaps you get pointers. Before I know what's happening, your mouth is around my cock, gliding up and down, the back of your throat embracing my cockhead. The bodies keep grinding even though there's no music, and my hands rest gently on the top of your head as you bob up and down on my cock.

When the lights go on a moment later, you're not the only one down on your knees. A few of the guys right around us see you and start to applaud and cheer. You come up for air and daintily shove my cock back into my pants. You don't bother to zip; instead, you just button the top button and put your arms around me.

"I'm sorry," you say. "When the lights went out, I just couldn't resist."

"No wonder the circuit breakers blew."

"Come upstairs with me," you say. "I know where there's an empty bedroom."

Half of me wants to button my pants, but the rest of me doesn't care. You lead me by the hand up a winding staircase to a long hall with hardwood floors. Guys are lip-locked in line for the bathroom. You push past them, fish in your skin-tight jeans and take out a key. You open one of the doors and a guy in line—one of the few without another guy feeling him up—says bitchily "Is there another bathroom in there?"

"Afraid not," you say, and drag me in.

It's totally dark in the room beyond. You lock the door behind us and shove me against it, dropping to your knees again. My cock is in your mouth even faster this time, and when I throw back my head and moan, you stand up quickly and kiss me. I can taste my own cock on your mouth. You guide me around as if you know the room intimately, and when you push me back I go tumbling onto a big, soft bed.

You're on top of me, kissing me, voracious. I reach up under your top and peel it off of you, discovering what I already knew—you're not wearing a bra. I press my mouth to your nipples and gently caress your tits while you writhe and moan on top of me. Just a few more strokes of your mouth and I'll come, but I don't want to come yet. Still sucking your tits, I push you onto your back and unbutton your jeans.

They're so tight that it takes some doing to get them peeled down your legs. They're damp, and so's your thong. My eyes are starting to adjust to the darkness, and I can see as I kiss my way up your legs that your pussy is shaved smooth. Not that I wouldn't have found out a moment later, anyway, as my tongue glides between your soft lips and strokes your clit. You're pierced there, too, and in a row down each cunt lip, three or perhaps four rings through each side of your shaved pussy.

Obviously, you know your rich queer friend from the Hollywood Boulevard side of Mulholland. But then, I already knew that.

You're on the huge bed edge-to-edge, instead of head-to-foot, so it's easy for me to drop to my knees and get a better angle at your hungry cunt. You lift your ass off the bed, moaning as I press hard into you.

My fingers slide into you easily, telling me just how wet you are—as if your soaked jeans and thong hadn't already told me. You're naked, now, writhing on my tongue, your thighs spread wide and your pussy opened for me. My eyes are finally opened to the semi-darkness. When I look up I see your glorious body stretched out before me, white in the moonlight from a nearby window, tits gathered in one hand, the other gently caressing the top of my head. You're looking down at me, your mouth hanging open and glistening moist like your eyes. Your blonde hair is swept in big messy strands around your face, neck and tits. You're gorgeous, and I can see just how close you are to coming.

I can also see the guy standing in the nearby doorway. Beyond, it looks like there's a bathroom, lit only by candle-light. But with the moonlight, and my eyes adjusted, I can see him pretty clearly—he's older, suit-clad, silver-haired, and I do recognize him. He's a screenwriter and actor, British, famously unmarried, famously eccentric. Everyone knows he's queer, except, of course, for everyone.

Jacob is watching us intently.

"Oh, don't stop on my account," he says. "After all, the door was locked, you naughty kids."

"I'm sorry, we—" I begin.

You're so close to coming that it takes you a moment to register the voice. Your head twists around and you look back at him.

"Jacob," you say hoarsely. "I didn't see you."

"Hello, there, Suzanne. Having a good night, I hope?"

You start to slide out from under me, but he puts up his hands.

"Please, don't stop. As long as you don't mind me here, you're welcome to use the bed. That doesn't bother you, does it?"

You look down at me, guiltily, scared, like you're expecting me to run screaming. From downstairs, I can just hear the pounding rhythm of "O Chanukah."

"Not even a little bit," I say. "Watch away."

Jacob laughs. "Must be another actor," he says. "She needs very badly to come. You can see it in her eyes. You must be really quite good with that tongue of yours. Isn't that right, Suzanne?"

"He's great," you say, your voice breathy.

"Then by all means. Give the poor girl what she wants. We've been friends far too long for me to stand in her way."

My cock is throbbing hard against the edge of the bed, and I'm still hungry for your pussy. I lower my face and press my tongue between your lips again, and you gasp and claw at the bed as I begin to lick in earnest.

Jacob watches, fascinated, as you hover on the edge of orgasm. I lick faster and you moan, your back arching—it only takes a moment to drive you over the edge. My two fingers inside you feel the tightening as you get close, and when I try to slide three in there I discover that Hollywood girls do their Kegels. You almost squeeze my fingers out when you come, and you all but box my ears as you shudder all over and your thighs quiver tight, closed against my head. Your ass is lifted so high off the bed I have to tuck my arm under you to keep my mouth on your clit. Nothing like a little Hollywood Fitness to keep a girl limber.

"Very, very good," says Jacob. "You're really quite adept at that. Isn't he, Suzanne?"

"Fuck me," you gasp, sitting up fast and pushing my head out from between your legs. "Please. Fuck me?"

I want to fuck you more than I've ever wanted to do anything in my life. I look up at Jacob. "By all means," he says. "She's certainly earned it."

I'm on you in an instant, your hands hungrily stripping my shirt off and pulling my jeans down over my ass. Your nails dig into me as I enter you, and you come again just as I start to thrust. I kiss you hard and feel your tongue, still tasting of my cock, still urging me forward. I fuck you harder, lifting your legs over my shoulders, bent at the knees, giving myself just the angle I like. I reach down and touch your clit as I drive into you, and you come a third time before I let myself go inside you. I've pushed you back across the bed, so intent on fucking you that I didn't realize you're hanging halfway over the edge, only your ass supporting you. As my spent cock slides out of you, we both go tumbling onto the floor. We would both giggle if we weren't still breathing too hard.

I lay there, sprawled on the floor, limbs tangled with yours. Jacob walks over and politely kneels down next to us; you look up at him, your face a mixture of embarrassment and excitement. With a good deal of post-orgasmic dullness mixed in.

Jacob leans down and kisses you on the lips, gently, not a sexual kiss—paternal, friendly, kind, affectionate. He strokes your sweaty, tangled blonde hair and says "Well done, my dear. It's good to see you dating again."

Then, without asking, he leans over you and kisses me, once, on the lips, at first equally paternal, equally kind. I don't stop him, but I do notice his tongue grazing my lower lip in the instant before he pulls away.

Then he strokes my hair a little.

"You are an actor, aren't you?" he asks. "Suzanne does tend to favor actors."

"Screenwriter, actually," I tell him. "Well, novelist. But working on a screenplay."

His business card is already in his hand.

"I'd love to read it," he tells me, and gives me his card.

Then he leans down and gives you another kiss, this one slightly less paternal—and more, you might say, friendly.

"Thanks for bringing your new boyfriend over," he says. "Hope you enjoy the party."

He stands up, brushes himself off, smiles down at you, and blows me a kiss.

He vanishes into what I assumed was the bathroom, and I hear his footsteps across the floor on the other side.

We don't say a word as we dress and make our way down through the grinding male bodies and the opulent front yard. I open the passenger door for you and go to get in my side. You stop me and put your hand at the base of my neck, your body tentatively close to mine—barely touching this time, not close like before.

"Are you mad?" you ask.

I smile.

"Do you know how hard it is to get someone to read your screenplay in this town?"

"I'll read it," you say meekly.

I lean forward and kiss you—gently at first, then harder, tasting your tongue.

"I'd like that," I tell you, and walk around to the driver's side as the pulsing strains of "Rudolph the Red-Nosed Reindeer" throb temptingly up the long Mercedes-packed driveway.

Naughty or Nice?
Alison Tyler

On Christmas morning, Dillon woke me up with one arm wrapped tight around my waist, spooning me from behind. His body was warm, and I could feel that he was hard already. "Naughty or nice?" he murmured.

I responded with a query of my own, rolling over to look into his dark-blue eyes. "Do you even have to ask?"

"No, baby. But what do you think Santa had to say? You think there's a lump of coal waiting for you?"

I slid my hand under the blanket, touching him through his drawstring pants. "Doesn't feel like coal," I grinned. Dillon pulled away. Yes, he was hard, but he wasn't ready. Instead, he lifted a present from next to the bed. "Unwrap it," he instructed, "and then meet me in the living room."

He left before I could say a word. Excited by the surprise, I pushed myself up and tore off the paper, revealing Christmas clothes of the traditional variety—traditional slut, that is: red-marabou trimmed nightie, matching high-heeled slippers, panties with three rows of ruffles on the seat. I brought the new clothes to the bathroom, freshened up, and then headed out to the living room, where Dillon was already waiting.

Stockings hung from the mantle, filled with hidden secrets. Old classics played on the stereo. The white lights on the tree twinkled. And then there was Dillon. Aside from the weather, a sunny L.A. December, my Santa was the only nontraditional item in the scene. He didn't go for a red felt suit or white beard. Instead, he had on his standard casual clothes—black drawstring pants, black T-shirt, cranberry-colored cashmere V-neck—but he was wearing a red hat with a white trim.

"Look under the tree…"

I turned away from Dillon to look at the stash awaiting me: various-size packages wrapped in shiny metallic paper. Flushed with anticipation, I opened the one on the top, pulling out a set of cherry-red leather cuffs with gleaming silver hardware. Next up was a wooden paddle, with red and white stripes painted in a diagonal pattern. And there was more… toys in different decadent lengths. Plugs. Clamps. Dillon had clearly gone all out at the sex toy shop.

"See, Santa knew you'd been naughty," Dillon told me. "But he left the punishment up to me. Come on over here, bad girl, and bring that paddle with you."

I scrambled to his side, paddle in my hands, embarrassed at how ready I was to take the spanking but desperate as always to feel that first thrilling sting. Dillon draped me over his lap, positioning me so that my pussy pressed deliciously against his knee, and lifted the nightie. He used the paddle on me through my silly ruffled panties for the first few blows, and then set down the cruel device in order to pull those panties to my knees. I trembled at the feel of his fingertips on my skin as he traced designs over my naked cheeks. And then he lifted that candy-cane paddle and resumed the spanking.

"Now, tell me," he instructed between blows. "Tell me all the naughty things you did this year."

This caught me off guard. I couldn't think of all the naughty things I'd done in a week. How could I confess to a year's worth of sins? The paddle slammed against me. Dillon didn't like it when I made him wait.

"I don't know," I murmured, feeling tearful, but still completely blank. What had I done? What did he want to hear? What did Dillon consider naughty?

"Come on, Nic, if you confess, I'll help you wipe the slate clean for the new year…"

But I couldn't, not when upended over my stern man's lap. I wished I was able to paint a fantasy the way Dillon could—so effortlessly sliding into the role of the Christmas inquisitor, demanding my obedience, punishing me for each second that I made him wait.

"Then I'll help you," Dillon said, smacking me three times in a row so that I kicked out against him, my mules flying across the room. "You lost yourself in twisted little fantasies, didn't you?"

"Yes, sir." That was true enough.

"You touched yourself several times a day, coming so hard when you imagined filthy degrading situations. Right?"

"Yes, sir."

"You used the nozzle in the shower, pressed against your little clit, to get yourself off. You used a variety of toys, sliding them inside your pussy or your asshole. You dirty little girl. And you let your man do things to you that you wouldn't even tell your best friend about, am I right?"

"Oh, God, yes…"

"You should get coal in your stockings, shouldn't you?"

"No…"

The paddle was suddenly merciless, slamming through the air against me… Dillon didn't seem to want me to disagree with him. But what he said was wrong. "If I behaved all the time, you'd never have a reason to spank me."

He laughed at that. "Is that what you think, Nicola? Really? I'd always have a reason to spank you. Just look at you…" he pushed me off his lap and spread me out on the sofa, pulling my panties down to my ankles and then spreading my pussy lips apart with his fingertips. "Look how wet you get. I could spank you just because of that. Because it makes you wet. Nothing else makes you wet like this, does it? If that's not proof that you're naughty to the core, then I don't know what is."

I held my breath. Spread open like that, with Dillon's breath warm on my wet skin, I felt on the verge of coming. But I wasn't sure at all of what Dillon had in mind. He pulled the hat off, then bent down and started to lick me, so gently that I felt myself falling. How could he spank me so hard one moment and then treat me like this the next? I couldn't fathom. But I didn't fight. I closed my eyes as he tricked his tongue in those magical spirals. I gripped his shoulders through the soft fabric of his sweater, holding him to me, silently begging him to let me climax once before he switched gears. Because knowing Dillon, this wouldn't be the only item on the menu for the morning. Not with the rest of the boxes still wrapped under the tree. Not with the…

"Go get the stocking," he said, pulling away before I reached that perfect moment. I blinked several times, trying to regain my sense of self before I reached for the panties. "No, you can take those all the way off." I kicked them away, then padded half-naked to the mantle and reached for the stocking. I didn't open it or peek. I brought the thing back to Dillon, who immediately pulled out red and green clothespins. So festive! So flirty! So fucking painful when he clipped the first one onto me, ultimately decorating my pussy lips with a series of the vibrantly colored clips. Next up were nipple clamps, and Dillon undid the tie of the sheer robe himself, fastening the clamps to my rock-hard nipples, making sure the clamps wouldn't move when he tugged on the chain.

I was lost in a whirlwind of pain, but Dillon knew what to do. Back he went, his tongue resuming those decadent spirals around my clit. And once more I found myself on the brink, teetering, almost....

But no.

Without warning, Dillon flipped me over, face down on the sofa, and reached for the new cuffs. In moments, he had my wrists bound over my head, and then he was shoving the marabou-trimmed robe out of the way, parting the cheeks of my ass, and sliding in one of the new plugs—as robustly red as the globe ornaments on our tree.

"What's that, baby doll?" Dillon crooned, leaning his head toward me.

I hadn't realized I was making any noise until Dillon spoke. But I had been moaning, wordlessly begging for him to have pity.

"Please, Dillon. Please let me..."

"Oh, you'll come," Dillon promised me. "But not yet."

And then he was up once more, rummaging behind the tree for a long, slim package, ripping off the wrapping himself to reveal a brand-new crop. Red, with green ribbons tied to the handle. He was a slave to the Christmas spirit, if nothing else.

"There's twelve days of Christmas, isn't that right?"

I couldn't speak. I couldn't think. I could hardly breathe. But somehow I managed to nod.

"And if I have my traditions down, then I believe the first day is Christmas, and that the twelve days go forward into the first week of January."

I nodded again, not sure what I was nodding to or why Dillon was talking about traditions.

"So twelve is the number for today," Dillon continued. "Count them for me."

And with that, he positioned me bent over the arm of the sofa, and started. The crop a blur, the pain exploding through my body. I did my best, lost in a red haze of pain and pleasure. I was able to keep up, but barely. Desperate when Dillon finally dropped the crop and slid down his slacks, thrusting inside me with the same intensity with which he'd punished me—fucking me so hard and tugging on the chain running between my breasts to add to the rhythm of his movements. I felt almost as if I were lost in a dream. I'd barely had time to wake up before he'd started. And now look at me. Just look at me.

Ever the gentleman, Dillon brought one hand to my pussy just before he came, pinching my clit so that I would climax first. And he finished a beat later, letting my body embrace him, tighten on him, as he sealed himself to me.

The glittery lights from the Christmas tree filled my eyes as Dillon pulled out, as he spread me back out on the sofa, removing the clips and the clamps. And as he flipped me for a moment to pull out the plug, and then undid the cuffs and carried me in his arms to the bathroom, I had one last look at the living room—at the wreckage of Christmas we'd left behind. The torn papers. The sex toys scattered about.

Merry fucking Christmas. That's what it truly was.

About the Authors

Lisette Ashton is a UK author who has published more than two dozen erotic novels and countless short stories. Lisette writes principally for Virgin's Nexus imprint, as well as occasionally for the CP label Chimera Publishing. Lisette Ashton's stories have been described by reviewers as "no-holds-barred naughtiness" and "good dirty fun."

Tenille Brown's writing is featured online and in several print anthologies including *Caught Looking, Ultimate Lesbian Erotica 2007, Iridescence, A Is for Amour, D Is for Dress-Up,* and *The Greenwood Encyclopedia of African American Women Writers.* She obsessively shops for shoes, hats, and purses and keeps a daily blog on her website, www.tenillebrown.com.

Rachel Kramer Bussel (www.rachelkramerbussel.com) is the editor or co-editor of over a dozen anthologies, including *Caught Looking, Hide and Seek, He's on Top, She's on Top, Cross-dressing, Naughty Spanking Stories from A to Z 1* and *2,* and the nonfiction collection *Best Sex Writing 2008. Yes, Sir* and *Yes, Ma'am* will be published in early 2008. Her own erotica has been published in over a hundred anthologies, including *Best American Erotica 2004* and *2006,* and she's written for *Bust, Cosmo UK, Mediabistro, New York Post, San Francisco Chronicle,* and other publications. She hosts and curates In The Flesh Erotic Reading Series and wrote the popular "Lusty Lady" column for *The Village Voice.*

T.C. Calligari lives on the West Coast in British Columbia, Canada. T.C. has written in many genres and published fiction, poetry, and articles in such publications as *Descant, Amazing, ON Spec, Talebones, Chizine, Twilight Tales, Vestal Review, Northern Frights 4, Opulence Magazine,* and *Dreams of Decadence.* Previous erotica has been published in the *Guilty Pleasures, Erotic Fantasy* anthologies, and the Cleis books *B Is for Bondage* and *E Is for Exotic.* An erotic novel is also in the works.

Andrea Dale's stories have appeared in *Got a Minute?, C Is for Coeds,* and *Ultimate Lesbian Erotica 2007,* and on Fishnetmag. com. With co-authors, she has sold novels to Cheek Books (*A Little Night Music,* Sarah Dale) and Black Lace Books (*Cat Scratch Fever,* Sophie Mouette). She lives in Southern California within scent of the ocean and can sometimes be persuaded to bake at Christmas. Her website is at www.cyvarwydd.com.

Shanna Germain has to admit she has never sat on Santa's lap, although she'd sure like to someday—she has a feeling he knows how to deliver the goods! Shanna's work has been widely published in places like *Best American Erotica, Best Bondage Erotica, Caught Looking, Cowboy Lover, F Is for Fetish,* and *Salon.* You can learn more about her (and see what she's asking Santa for this year) at www.shannagermain.com.

Michelle Houston has been writing erotica since 1995 and has had stories published in many anthologies, including *D Is For Dress-Up, Naughty Stories from A to Z vol. 4, Three-way, Naughty Spanking Stories from A to Z vol. 2, The Happy Birthday Book of Erotica, C Is For Coeds,* and *Slave to Love.* In addition to her print publications, she also has several of her own e-books and stories in a couple other e-books. You can find out more about her and her writings on her personal website, The Erotic Pen (www.eroticpen.net).

Michael Hemmingson is a Zen Buddhist who lives near the beach in San Diego, California, and has written many Blue Moon Books, like *House of Dreams* and *Las Vegas Quartet.* His first indie film, *The Watermelon,* is in postproduction.

Joel A. Nichols was born and raised in Vermont. His stories will appear in *Distant Horizons, Sex by the Book: Gay Men's Tales of Lit and Lust, Travelrotica 2,* and *Second Skin,* and have appeared in *C is for Coeds, Dorm Porn 2, Full Body Contact, Just the Sex, Ultimate Undies,* and *Sexiest Soles.* An excerpt from his novel in progress won second place in the Brown Foundation Short Fiction Prize 2005. In 2002, he was a Fulbright Fellow in Berlin. Joel studied German at Wesleyan University and has a Creative Writing M.A. from Temple University. He lives in Philadelphia with his boyfriend, works at an Internet video company, and teaches college English. Visit www.joelanichols.com.

Jean Roberta teaches English in a university in the heart of Canada where the Royal Canadian Mounted Police have their headquarters. Over fifty of her erotic stories have appeared in print anthologies such as the annual *Best Lesbian Erotica* (2000–01 and every year since 2004), *Merry XXXmas,* and *The Mammoth Book of Best New Erotica 6.* Her stories and reviews also appear on websites such as Ruthie's Club, Clean Sheets, The Dominant's View, The Shadow Sacrament, Girlphoria, and TCM Reviews.

Teresa Noelle Roberts's erotica has appeared or is forthcoming in *B Is for Bondage; E Is for Exotic; F Is for Fetish; H Is for Hardcore; Chocolate Flava 2; Best Women's Erotica 2004, 2005,* and *2007; The Good Parts; Lipstick on Her Collar;* Fishnetmag.com; and many other publications. She is also half of the erotica-writing team called Sophie Mouette, author of *Cat Scratch Fever.*

Thomas S. Roche's relationship with Christmas has been a rocky one for some years; intermittently, he hosts the not-quite-annual Christmas Sucks reading series in San Francisco, where horrible and wonderful things happen to Santa Claus, Mrs. Claus, and various elves and reindeer. Between these occurrences, he hosts Dr. Sketchy's Barbary Coast, the mid–Left Coast incarnation of the national burlesque figure-drawing salon, Dr. Sketchy's Anti Art School. He also writes short stories, articles, and the occasional novel, teaches with San Francisco Sex Information (www.sfsi.org) and edits biweekly events, news, and reviews network Eros Zine (www.eroszine.com). Information about his events, articles, stories, and educational work can be found at www.thomasroche.com.

Dominic Santi is a former technical editor turned rogue whose stories have appeared in many dozens of anthologies and magazines, including the recent *His Underwear, Caught Looking, Bi Guys, Best Gay Erotica 2007,* and *Best of the Best Gay Erotica 2.* Santi's latest book is the German collection *Buddy Action.* Future plans include more dirty short stories and an even dirtier historical novel.

Savannah Stephens Smith lives and writes on Vancouver Island. Her current projects include taming a wild garden, training a willful dog, and writing a novel. She is currently stuck on the blackberry bushes, "sit," and chapter seven. Her previous fiction has appeared both online and in print. She's an alto who's been caught singing into her hairbrush, and rumor has it she laughs in her sleep. The only thing she likes more than writing is reading.

Brooke Stern is a Jew who goes to movies and writes books on Christmas. These books include *Suffering the Consequences* and *Bad Girls.* Stern has also written many stories, which have appeared in collections like *Naughty Spanking Stories from A to Z volume 2, A Is for Amour, C Is for Coeds, Got a Minute,* and *Love at First Sting* and on websites like Salon.com and Cleansheets.com. The original Victorian erotica that inspired "Everything You Need on Christmas" can be found in Stern's *The Collector's Edition of Victorian Erotic Discipline.*

Donna George Storey likes to indulge herself in all sorts of special solstice pleasures when the nights are longest. Her erotic fiction has appeared in *She's on Top, He's on Top, E Is for Exotic, Love at First Sting, Garden of the Perverse,*

Taboo, Best American Erotica 2006, Mammoth Book of Best New Erotica 4, 5, and *6,* and *Best Women's Erotica 2005, 2006,* and *2007.* Her novel set in Japan, *Amorous Woman,* is part of Orion's Neon erotica series. Read more of her work at www.DonnaGeorgeStorey.com.

Saskia Walker's erotic fiction appears in over forty anthologies, including *Caught Looking, She's on Top, Slave to Love, Secrets volume 15, The Mammoth Book of Best New Erotica volume 5, Stirring Up a Storm,* and *Kink.* She is the author of several novellas as well as the erotic novels *Along for the Ride, Double Dare,* and *Reckless.* Please visit www.saskiawalker.co.uk for more information.

Sharon Wachsler lives in rural New England with her partner and service dog. Her work has appeared in dozens of periodicals and books, including *Best American Erotica 2004* and *2005.* In 2006, the Astraea Foundation named Sharon an "Emerging Lesbian Writer" in fiction. Recent anthology credits include *Periphery, Bed,* and *Lipstick on Her Collar.* She is the founder, editor, and humor columnist of Breath & Shadow (abilitymaine.org/breath) and is compiling her Sick Humor essays and cartoons into a book, *Sick Humor: Full-Frontal Disability.* To get on her mailing list, email sickhumor2@aol.com or visit her at sharonwachsler.com or sickhumorpostcards.com.

About the Editor

Called "a trollop with a laptop" by *East Bay Express,* and a "literary siren" by Good Vibrations, **Alison Tyler** is naughty and she knows it. (And so does Santa.) Ms. Tyler is the author of more than twenty-five explicit novels, including *Learning to Love It, Strictly Confidential, Sweet Thing, Sticky Fingers, Something About Workmen, Rumors, Tiffany Twisted,* and *With or Without You* (Cheek). Her short stories have appeared in more than seventy anthologies and have been translated into Spanish, German, Italian, Japanese, Greek, and Dutch.

She is the editor of thirty-five anthologies, including *Batteries Not Included* (Diva) and *Naughty Fairy Tales from A to Z* (Plume) as well as the *Naughty Stories from A to Z* series, the *Down & Dirty* series, *Naked Erotica,* and *Juicy Erotica* (all from Pretty Things Press). Please visit www.prettythingspress.com.

Ms. Tyler is loyal to coffee (black), lipstick (red), and tequila (straight). She has tattoos but no piercings, a wicked tongue but a quick smile, and bittersweet memories but no regrets. She believes it won't rain if she doesn't bring an umbrella, prefers hot and dry to cold and wet, and loves to spout her favorite motto: "You can sleep when you're dead." She chooses Led Zeppelin over the Beatles, the Cure over the Smiths, and the Stones over everyone—yet although she appreciates good rock, she has a pitiful weakness for eighties hair bands.

In all things important, she remains faithful to her partner of over a decade, but she still can't choose just one perfume.